A Realist in Eden

Harry Bodine

Copyright © 2022 by Harry Bodine

All rights reserved.

No part of this book may be reproduced in any form or by any electronic or mechanical means, including information storage and retrieval systems, without written permission from the author, except for the use of brief quotations in a book review.

Cover image: gerasimov174 / Adobe Stock, used with permission

This book is dedicated to Winona, the best wife and soulmate who ever lived, in appreciation of 61 years of love and steadfast loyalty.

Responsibility for the title goes to my friend Cody Stevens, who offered this thought while driving our blue Honda at age 16:

"I'm not an optimist. I'm not a pessimist. I AM a realist."

Chapter 1

How Far We Have Come

"James Cameron Bonner, do you solemnly pledge to defend the Charter of Rights of the Dominion of Columbia, guard its people from foreign aggression, protect the rights pledged to its citizens under the laws of the Dominion with all the power in your command, so help you God?"

"I do," James replied, his left hand resting on old King James Bible rescued from the ruins of a 19th century brick church leveled in the massive earthquake that had struck the west coast of North America ten years ago.

He smiled, shook Chief Justice Bruce Babbitt's hand and turned to face the podium and the crowd gathered in the Great Hall of Parliament, previously known as the University of Washington Huskies' basketball arena, Hec Edmunson Pavilion. With one fourth of the arena sealed off behind the podium, the 7,000 seats were filled with two prominent exceptions—chairs reserved for official representatives of the United States and Canada.

Adjusting the microphone to reflect his five-foot, eleven-inch body, James Bonner did not resemble a typical head of state. His blond hair close clipped, his mid-30s body showing no signs of a

1

paunchy stomach, he resembled a man who spent his working days outdoors, not a political administrator taking on a new four-year assignment of running a newly formed country.

James was taking the oath as governor of the Dominion of Columbia a second time. As he adjusted the microphone, he recalled taking the same oath four years earlier in a cold underground parking garage near the Washington State Capitol, the site chosen because its roof did not leak.

His thoughts raced for a moment over the last four years in which he had led his newly found country—never intended to be a long-term government—through some major crises. He and his Realist Party had been rewarded richly in an election a month earlier. Now his friends in Parliament who had supported him and leaders of the "loyal opposition" whom he had trounced in the election sat in a large semicircle in front of him along with justices of the High Court and his family. Behind them were ranged members of the general public. They expected him to list goals he wanted the Dominion to achieve in his second term that started with this ceremony. He did exactly that.

James Bonner was no orator. He never was truly comfortable being the center of attention. As was his style he spoke slowly. His sentences short, he spelled out his goals one-two-three-four in a talk that, according to custom, never lasted longer than 20 minutes.

First and foremost, the Dominion would continue rebuilding its infrastructure damaged beyond recognition by the August 1 earthquake that hit the coast and interior valleys east of the Coast Range. It would continue to be a slow gradual process, but the task would be pursued as fast as possible as money became available.

The Dominion would also continue monitoring riots and unrest still wracking California to the south. California border crossings would remain closed until California really calmed down. It also would continue to seek a peaceful relationship with the world's greatest military and naval power, China, whose diplomats had offered to protect Columbia and its residents as they rebuilt their cities and small towns. Negotiations with the Chinese would go forward with the understanding that any eventual decision would not compromise the Dominion's right to exist as a free nation. Columbia would not become a satellite in a new Chinese world order.

He would ask the new Parliament to continue simplifying tax laws which needed greater clarity and many revisions. Most of the tax code, dating back to the previous US and Canadian governments, granted too many privileges to some and penalized too many others.

Barring another calamity like the earthquake or an attack by a foreign power, he would seek balanced budgets and veto any bills creating debt. He also would seek ways to help those who lost everything in the quake's aftermath of the quake.

While delivering his talk, James looked down to the front row in front of the podium where his wife, Lisa, sat with their two children, Lori, now 13, and Skip, 12.

How far both they as a family and his cobbled together country between the Pacific Ocean and Rocky Mountains had come in the 10 years since the Cascadian subduction earth- quake had demolished the physical world in which they lived. The quake had been followed by the collapse of the US government in a convulsion of riots and mayhem finally crushed by the armed forces. A military junta now ruled, but so far had not sought to impose its will in the Pacific Northwest.

The political implosion of the United States was matched by the death of the world economic order previously built around the mighty American dollar and American military power. Now most of North America and the rest of the world were trying to construct a new world order amidst revolution, famine and multiple wars.

James smiled at Lisa. She and Lori smiled back. Skip raised his right hand from his lap and flashed a thumbs up at his father on the podium. He and Skip, whose real name was Michael, but known to both family and friends since he was a toddler as Skip, shared a strong bond.

All four of them knew that when today's ceremonies were over, they would be going to the Selkirk Mountains in British Columbia to snowboard for three days, a long deferred vacation. Three days of solitude in a mountain cabin. Two security officers would be close, but not in their faces. It would be a time to relax, enjoy each other's company without interruption and to simply have fun.

Fun, James thought, vacation time, a concept unknown to millions around the world. In Columbia it. was starting to happen again, a glimpse of the return of normalcy to life.

James concluded his second inaugural talk with an announcement no one in his audience expected.

"As I begin a second four-year term as governor of Columbia, I want everyone to know this will be my last term. Four years from now I will leave government and turn Columbia over to my successor who hopefully will lead Columbia, free, into an even better future."

He remained at the podium as the entire assembly stood for the national anthem, a spinoff of "America the Beautiful." He then turned and greeted those gathered on the platform around him, Assembly Speaker David Owen, Council President Diana Faulk, the High Court justices, Washington Governor Del Williams and Seattle Mayor Peter Chang.

All in all it was a good start for his second round as the head of a government, insignificant as it was among all the nations of the world.

* * *

"WHAT WAS IT LIKE, DAD?" ANOTHER QUESTION FROM HIS SON, always curious about a world he had never known, but within the memory of everyone over the age of 15. The old days when the United States was a world power with an army, navy and air force respected and feared across the globe. The old days with 280 million cars in North America, unlimited computer games, airliners that could whisk common people to Europe or Asia within hours. The old days with running water, toilets that always worked, television channels beyond count and restaurants offering rare foods from every corner of the planet. Would they ever really come back?

That world was gone now. The pace of life was much slower. Skip watched his father, the leader of his country, splitting logs for the fire that would keep their cabin warm for the next 24 hours.

"Did everyone really have a car that could drive from ocean to ocean?" Skip asked. (Skip was an indifferent student, but he was fascinated by an old globe in his classroom at school).

"Most families had cars. Mine didn't," James replied, bringing the ax down with extra force as he tried to split a large log with a knot in it.

"We were poor," he added. "Much of the time we lived on food stamps and I remember we were often hungry. We moved a lot, going from relative to relative. Eventually they all got tired of us and asked us to leave.

"Why did they want you to go?" Skip asked.

"There were problems," James replied, bringing the ax down with a blow that the cut the stubborn piece of pine neatly in half. "Someday, when you are older, I'll tell you about my childhood. In the meantime, let's get this wood inside and see how Mom is coming with dinner."

He and Skip gathered several pieces of wood, pushed open the door of the cabin and dumped the load into a box next to the stone fireplace. After several trips the job was done. Father and son took off their heavy jackets and hung them on pegs next to the front door of the cabin.

Dinner was still in the future. Lisa and Lori were reading in the declining daylight that came through a large window facing west. The fire in the stove placed in the fireplace generated welcome warmth.

James heard a noise outside the cabin. Two men, bundled against the cold were snowshoeing up the hill. One of them, seeing James looking out the window, waved a greeting. Minutes later they parked their snowshoes outside the door and were welcomed into the cabin.

Daniel Carter and William Slavey were assigned to guard the Bonners on their holiday. Earlier in the day they had inspected the woods surrounding the cabin which faced southward and overlooked an open meadow leading to the valley below. They had contacted the one-man police department in the village at the lower end of the valley. The officer agreed to notify them if anything unusual, especially strangers showing up, occurred. The two guards had erected a rough open-sided shelter 100 yards down the hill in a spot that gave them a commanding view extending from the Bonner cabin to the end of the road in the village. They would sleep in shifts, one always awake to spot any danger that might appear.

One of the men kept looking out the window as the other visited with James and the family. Dinner appeared, a hearty stew of meat and vegetables. The first family and guards shared it. Later they stood guard while Bonners old and young put on boots and trudged through the snow to the two-seater outhouse 30 yards away. Back in the cabin Carter and Slavey made sure they and the Bonners had working battery-powered radios that could reach each other if needed. They then took their leave and snowshoed their way back down the hillside, the snow radiant under a full moon and cloudless sky.

Two days of bliss followed, snowboarding and sledding during the short daylight, dominoes and games in the warm, cozy cabin after dark.

Too soon the short vacation came to an end. The Bonners, Carter, and Slavey closed the closed the cabin and snowshoed down the mountain where a horse-drawn sleigh awaited them. It would take them down the valley to a Canadian Pacific Railway siding where the Dominion's VIP car was parked. The first westbound freight from Calgary would halt long enough to couple their car to the back of the train and haul them to Vancouver.

As they entered the village, they encountered a middle-aged man with a beard and a group of teenage boys. They were all taller than Skip who stood four feet seven.

"We're on our way to an ice hockey practice," the coach announced. "Would your son like to join us? We have an extra pair of skates."

Skip responded at once. He had never played ice hockey and was thrilled at the prospect. "Can I, Dad? Can I?" he pleaded.

"He'd love to, but we have a schedule to meet. A question for you. Where are the helmets for the players?"

"We don't have helmets. We prohibit blows above the waist. We have tried to get helmets but have had no luck at all."

"I think helmets are critical for the players' safety," James said.

He extended his right hand and shook the coach's gloved hand. "James Bonner. Your name?"

"Greg Jablonski, I each high school and middle school history and coach basketball. Ice hockey I coach for fun."

"Tell you what I'll do when we get back to Seattle," James said. "I will locate some helmets and ship them to you. How many do you need?"

"Ten would be great. Twelve would be better. We're really isolated up here, you know. If you find helmets, you can mail them to General Delivery at the post office here in the village. We'll be sure you get paid for them," Jablonski said.

They shook hands and the Bonners boarded a horse drawn sleigh for the six-mile trip down the valley to the waiting rail car.

"Skip," James said, "next time you'll get your ice hockey game. In the meantime, you will grow stronger and be better able to handle the big kids."

"Promise?" Skip asked.

"I promise. It will happen," James replied. He glanced at Lisa whose face indicated no enthusiasm for having her child pounded by hockey sticks or knocked down by older teenagers.

Their eyes met. "It's part of growing up," James said. He took her hand and squeezed it gently. She leaned forward and kissed him on the cheek.

Back in the office two days later James's staff launched a search for ice hockey helmets and found a dozen of them at a sporting goods store recently reopened in Bothell. He had them shipped north with no bill, but with a hand-written note enclosed on the Dominion governor's stationary.

"Hope your guys have a great season."

Chapter 2

The Invitation

Rain was falling outside the executive office's windows when James's long-time friend and scheduler Don Lawson walked into the room.

"Jim, something new has come up," Don said. "Your folks in Forest Grove want to celebrate the 10th anniversary of Sponge Meadows and they want you to be principal speaker for the event." Don always called James by his nickname when the two of them were alone.

"What's the date?" James asked.

"Saturday, July 18. They are hoping for good weather."

"Any chance of a foreign invasion?" James joked. "Reliving Sponge Meadows is the last thing I want to do. I really prefer to focus on the present and future, not dwell on the past."

"Jim, I think you're hooked," Don replied. "If you don't show up there could be real repercussions, none of them good."

James nodded in agreement. Politically, he had to go. "Let me talk it over with Lisa tonight and we will respond to the invitation tomorrow." He then asked Don to give him the latest developments on the budget Parliament was assembling and then an update on restoring the power grid. Thank God, that project was in its final redundancy phase.

At home that night he and Lisa discussed Sponge Meadows. They agreed. He had to make the trip and speak. She and the children also would go.

Later that night James was unable to sleep. He started composing his message, listing points that had to be made. In July he was still working on the message as the train carried them south to Portland and onto a branch line to Forest Grove. There the party switched to aging automobiles for the rest of the trip into the Coast Range.

Arriving at the site James was shocked at the size of the crowd. There had to be up to a thousand men, women and children standing or sitting in portable chairs gathered around hastily built wooden platform large enough for a dozen people. At noon the program began with the Forest Grove High School Band playing the national anthem. Then Oregon's governor, Gloria Martinez stepped forward to introduce James. She was brief. James stood behind the microphone, acknowledged the crowd and began his talk.

"Friends, we gather today at a placed where the darkest period of recent Pacific Northwest history came to an end. This place, Sponge Meadows, is where a vigilante group, of which I was a part, brought a reign of terror to its end by killing 32 men. It was not a battle. It was a massacre pour and simple and executed deliberately after very careful and thorough planning.

"We know the history. The 32 men were a motorcycle gang that terrorized the Willamette Valley over a period of several months. The gang attacked small high schools in rural settings. The gang assembled students in school gyms and raped selected students in front of their classmates. When some students or teachers tried to intervene they were gunned down by gang members guarding the exits and armed with Ak-47s. The carnage was horrible. The rapes if anything were worse.

"The gang, named the Malvadoes, marauded over a wide area. No one felt safe. Established law enforcement agencies, handicapped by power failures and setbacks caused by the earthquake, were unable to track down the gang who killed several outgunned sheriff's deputies who tried to stop them. Appeals to higher authorities drew no meaningful responses. The valley was gripped with fear. Could it happen here?

"In Forest Grove four friends sharing beers in a tavern one night started discussing possible ways the gang might be stopped. The only decision they reached that night was to meet again in a more private setting. They invited me to join them because one of the group understood I collected guns and enjoyed shooting them in target practices in an abandoned quarry west of town.

"Together we hatched a plot. We created a plan to draw the Malvadoes into a trap, an ambush. The spot we visit today is where it happened. Thirty-two gang members died here. They, their motorcycles, their clothing, their personal possessions were burned and buried in open fields just west of here. The five of us, reinforced by 25 gun owners recruited at the last minute, rid the Willamette Valley of a horrible menace.

"Are we heroes? No. Are we mass murderers as the last governor of Oregon believed? The answer might be called, charitably, justified mass homicide.

"So how should we handle this particular moment in our history? I would suggest we erect a small monument explaining what happened here and what caused it to happen.

"Beyond that we should focus on the future and build a society where a gang like the Malvadoes cannot create a reign of terror. That's the best gift we can give to those who follow us.

"Thank you."

James returned to his seat as Forest Grove Mayor Gretchen Noyes thanked him and dismissed the crowd to go home.

Suddenly a voice rang out from the crowd. "Question? Would Governor Bonner take a question?"

James immediately stood and returned to the podium. "What is your question?" he asked.

"Do you feel guilt for your role in the massacre?" the young man asked.

"Short answer, 'yes,' and thank you for asking. You have focused on the core of what Sponge Meadows is all about.

"Let me ask you a question. If you were in my shoes ten years ago and this motorcycle gang was threatening your son or daughter with rape, mutilation or death, would you act to stop them when those ultimately responsible did nothing? Or would you take action that went beyond the law and violated the gang's Constitutional rights?

"I made a decision. I organized their destruction. I would do the same thing again under the circumstances I faced at the time."

This time the crowd erupted with applause before continuing their way home.

A large number stayed around the platform to shake hands with James and thank him. Among them was Alex Martinez, his one-time business partner. The two men hugged and then reintroduced their families. The conversation was good until James remembered the Bonners had a train schedule to meet.

Finally alone, Lisa gave James a hug. "You were magnificent," she told her husband. "I'm very proud." Lori was up next. James got another hug. Finally, Skip got his turn, extending his right hand for a handshake.

"I'm glad you let me come today, Dad. I won't forget it. And I'm very proud you are my Dad."

Chapter 3

The Day the World Ended

Lying on the bed in the cordoned-off section of Columbia Railways' VIP car on the trip back to the capitol, James was unable to sleep. His mind reviewed the day's events and he wondered how the talk he had given at Sponge Meadows would be received east of the Cascades and in the Lower Mainland. Fortunately, Lisa and the children were fast asleep so, as he adjusted himself from time to time, he did not disturb them.

Suddenly he focused on how this entire adventure of the last 10 years had evolved. He and his business partner, Alex Martinez, were midway through building a house on Nineteenth Street on an infill lot in the oldest part of Forest Grove. Drywall would be the job of the coming day and he remembered looking at the alarm clock. It showed 4 a.m. so he had another hour before he had to get up. He wrapped his right arm around Lisa's waist and recalled the marvelous sex they had enjoyed after turning in the evening before.

Then it happened, the long-expected overdue Cascadian tectonic plate shifted off the central Oregon coast. First, there was a huge boom followed by their mobile home suddenly lurching to the right and sliding off its concrete block foundation.

He and Lisa were almost thrown off the bed as the walls twisted. The ceiling did not collapse. James tried to stand up, but another shift turned his legs to jelly and he fell to the floor. Outside he could see electricity arcing as lines were torn off poles. Sirens sounded in the distance, a mix of car and home alarms.

I have to shut off the gas, he thought, glad that both he and Lisa no longer smoked. Lisa also was awake and trying to crawl into the adjacent bedroom where baby Lori's bed had bounced across the room and now rested against the opposite wall. Lori was crying. Lisa carefully lifted her off the crib and cradled her in her arms as she sat on the floor.

James meanwhile found the connection box that linked the outside gas line to their furnace and turned the handle to close the valve. Then he saw his pickup truck pinned under a 12-inch diameter tree limb that landed on the edge of the cab and then rolled onto the box that held his tools. The box was ruined. I'll have to get to the chain saw and cut the tree away, he thought.

His cell phone rang. Damn, I should have recharged it last night, he thought as he opened the phone. It was Alex Martinez, his co-worker partner. Alex reported he and his girlfriend Rita were safe although the house they rented was now unlivable. James told him they should meet on Nineteenth Street after he freed his pickup and found a safe place for Lisa and Lori to stay. He then phoned his mother whose landline phone did not ring. He phoned his step-brother Al who lived closer to their mom and asked him to check up on her.

After that everything went downhill. The electricity was shut off as Bonneville Power's computers lay in a tangled mess in Vancouver and miles of towers and high-tension transmission lines fell to the ground. Even those linking The Dalles in Oregon to Sylmar, California, which ran east of the Cascades, collapsed at several locations north and south of Bend. The entire Northwest seemed to go dark except for a number of fires triggered by the downed lines before power was cut.

First things first. After checking on Lisa and Lori and asking Lisa to pack some clothes and important household documents, James started the chainsaw and liberated his aged pickup truck. He then loaded his wife and child and two suitcases into the truck and carefully picked his way around cracks and downed lines in the street and drove to Joseph Gale Elementary School which stood intact with its door open to a growing number of families who were seeking shelter.

Telling Lisa he would return after checking on the Nineteenth Street house, he made his way across town.

The trip took longer than he had anticipated. Blocked everywhere by slabs of uplifted asphalt and large sinkholes, he reached downtown where collapsed buildings surrounded the key Pacific Avenue-Main Street intersection. Even more distressing, he could see looters already busy at work.

Civilization is going down like a line of dominoes, James thought. Finally reaching the construction site on Nineteenth Street, James was relieved to see the house still stood and that it still had a roof. He was glad the owner, who lived in Indiana, had decided to anchor the house to the foundation to the structure, a recommendation seldom followed despite its playing a key role in keeping houses in one piece.

He phoned Alex. "Why don't we move in? There's plenty of room for the five of us and there is strength in numbers if someone challenges our using the house," he added, remembering the looters he had seen downtown. Alex agreed and said he and Lisa would be there in a few minutes.

Retrieving Lisa and Lori, he drove back to their destroyed home. Together they emptied the refrigerator and freezer and packed their contents into the truck bed along with clothing, cherished personal items, and some firewood from the fallen tree. After delivering Lisa back to Nineteenth Street and unloading all they had brought, James made one final trip to their former home.

Going to the bedroom, he forcibly opened a closet door which had frozen shut in the quake. Lifting a section of carpet, he raised a small door in the floor that opened to a crawl space and looked for a storage box.

He couldn't find it. Obviously, it had slid across the black plastic sheeting that served as a moisture barrier. Reaching for his cell phone, he turned on the mag light and shined it around in a circle, finally spotting the box on the far side of the house.

Noting the direction, he left the bedroom and walked to the far side of the living room, knelt, and, using a hacksaw, cut another hole in the carpet and floor. Ten minutes later he lifted the waterproof box into the living room and opened it. Inside, he found three rifles and a shotgun along with boxes of ammunition. He then reloaded the box, relocked it and carried it to the passenger seat in the pickup and drove back to Nineteenth Street.

That evening the Bonners and Martinezes thawed the frozen food, cooked it over an open fire in the backyard and feasted on the contents before they thawed and spoiled. A few neighbors they had not met before joined them and helped them devour a banquet of meats, vegetables, fruits, milk and ice cream. Everyone present wound up stuffed. They all would long remember that night when they gorged on food, a stark contrast to the months of ongoing hunger that followed.

The next day James bought the last gasoline Forest Grove would see for months and he and Alex dug a latrine and built an outhouse in the backyard. James then helped Lisa place the furniture they had brought with them. Finally they spent an hour teaching Lisa how to load and shoot a 30.06. The world had changed beyond imagining and he wanted Lisa prepared to handle dangers that might lay ahead.

Chapter 4

Ultimate Surprise

AN UNUSUALLY WARM FALL NIGHT HAD BOTH JAMES AND LISA sleeping restlessly. James's mind wandered until it locked on one of the unforeseen impacts of the post-earthquake era, which at the outset was compounded by the depletion of the Social Security Trust Fund's reserve and an immediate 45% drop in monthly automatic deposits to 100 million Social Security recipients' accounts. That had led to a societal meltdown across the nation and was followed by riots in many large cities along with a cascading economic collapse from coast to coast.

That was not on James's thoughts as he half dozed. His mind focused on a shortage no one had anticipated—the vanishing of condoms. Because Lisa had had major complications and a major loss of blood when Lori was born, her gynecologist, Martha Ide, had warned her a second pregnancy might be fatal and should be avoided at all costs. The disappearance of condoms from store shelves ended the sex Lisa and James so enjoyed. Other birth control measures still threatened risk so sex came to an end until condoms became available.

A sudden noise from the front of the house instantly refocused

James's mind. He reached over, turned a key in a drawer of a side stand and reached inside for the pistol he stored there when he was sleeping. Quietly, he pulled the sheet back and rose from the bed and then made his way to the front of the house. Easing up to a window he gazed out at the porch.

All was quiet. He was certain the noise he had heard had come from the porch, but no one was in sight and the street in both directions from the house was empty and quiet. He then checked windows on both sides of the house and the backyard. Seeing nothing, he returned to the bedroom, put the gun back in the drawer, locked it and slowly eased into the bed where Lisa still slept.

James did not hear the next unusual sound, but Lisa did. It sounds like a baby crying or whimpering, she thought.

Slipping on a robe, she went to the front of the house and quietly opened the front door a crack. Immediately she spotted a small box, a little bigger than a shoebox, wedged against the door. Lisa eased the box over the sill and into the living room, closed the door and peered inside. It was a baby, wrapped in a large bath towel. The movement had fully awakened it and now it bawled.

Lisa looked up and saw James had joined her, standing barefoot and wearing only the shorts he liked to sleep in.

Lisa reached into the box, pulled the towel aside and lifted the baby out, suddenly encountering a loose-fitting diaper wet from urine and oozing with shit. She took the now-squalling baby to the kitchen and placed it on the counter next to the sink. James followed with the box, placing it on a chair for a closer examination later.

Lisa positioned the baby away from the edge so it could not fall to the floor. James stirred embers of the fire in the kitchen stove in an effort to restore some heat to the room and begin warming up a kettle of water to clean the baby.

Reaching for a dishcloth, Lisa began cleaning up the baby's mess, carefully removing hardened feces from its backside.

"It's a boy," she said. The infant continued to wail and Lisa wondered what she could feed it. She recalled she had used the last of the milk stored in the ice box the night before.

Finding a towel, she wrapped the baby in it. Cradling the baby in her left arm, she opened a cabinet door and pulled out a can of chicken broth. James opened the broth and poured its contents into a small pan which he had placed on the top of the slowly warming stove. He then turned his attention to the small cardboard box and emptied it, placing the dirty soiled towel on the floor. Turning the box over he examined the bottom and sides looking for some clue that might identify where it came from. The only thing he found was a mailing label—"Ace Hardware"—with an address on West Baseline in Hillsboro, the county seat.

Lisa meanwhile rewrapped the baby and retrieved a spoon, offering sips of the now-warm broth to the infant. It took just a second for the baby to understand he was being offered nourishment. He sucked on the plastic spoon and swallowed the broth. The kid no longer was starving and now was both warm and comfortable. The crying stopped.

James and Lisa looked into each other's eyes in the dim light of the kitchen.

"Do we suddenly have a son?" she asked.

"I don't know, but we have to report this to the police and find out if anyone is missing a baby. We don't have a choice," James said.

In the days that followed James contacted the Forest Grove police who in turn notified the county sheriff's office and the state's Child Services agency. He also placed handbills on bulletin boards around town, a process that took days since travel was still primarily by bicycle or walking.

Lisa and James had taken the baby to see Dr. William Young, Forest Grove's elderly, but still practicing pediatrician. Other than a rash on its butt caused by delays in changing diapers, he pronounced the kid healthy. He thought the baby was a month or two old at the most.

"What's his name?" Dr. Young asked.

"We haven't gotten around to that," Lisa replied. "We're trying to find out if someone is missing a baby."

"He needs a name," Young replied, "and don't be surprised if no one comes forward. The way he arrived on your front porch makes me feel he or she wanted you two to have this baby."

Ten days after the baby appeared on their front porch, a social worker appeared the Bonners' door, came in, introduced herself and examined the baby. For once it was quiet and content after a feeding a short time before. James had resurrected a crib and playpen that Lori, now walking, had used in her infancy.

The social worker explained that foster homes were exceedingly hard to find in the aftermath of the earthquake.

"Can you and your husband continue to take care of him?" she asked.

"We'd love to. I keep praying no one will show up to claim him," Lisa replied.

"Well for now that appears to be the best option for the baby. I'll recommend to the health department that this boy stay with you," she said. "I'll file my report. Unless something comes up, the department will check back with you in a month or two."

When James returned home after a day at his latest construction site, Lisa reported the social worker's visit and her recommendation that the baby stay with them for the time being.

After a lot of discussion, Lisa and James decided to name the baby after their grandfathers Henry and Michael. That did not stick. Henry Michael gave way to a nickname, Skip. The decision was Lori's. The name Skip came from a child's book Lisa had checked out from the Forest Grove Library. The story featured a young girl and her cocker spaniel dog. Its name was Skip and Lori started calling her infant brother "Skip."

Lori, almost two, watched her mother bathe and feed Skip and tried to imitate her mother's actions. She was very happy when Lisa placed Skip on the couch and let her cradle him in her arms. After three months he seldom cried unless he wanted food or attention and the family settled into a routine. All four were happy. The social workers's visits became less frequent, while at the same time notices about Skip that James had posted around town drew no strangers to the Bonners' front door claiming ownership.

James carefully kept the box Skip had arrived in, wrapping it in an old tattered blanket and storing it in the back of the closet above the crawl space where he stored his guns. After eight months passed, he and Lisa had a conversation one night: Should they initiate a formal adoption process for Skip who continued to thrive in their home?

James and Lisa consulted a lawyer in Hillsboro and six weeks later they stood in a courtroom facing Judge Nan Turnbull. The hearing was brief. No one appeared to oppose the adoption. Judge Turnbull signed the needed documents, a copy of which was posted in a sealed glass case next to the courthouse's front door. State law was satisfied. The Bonners were overjoyed. They had both a daughter and a son.

Chapter 5

Eternal Winter, Glimmer of Spring

THE FIRST WINTER AFTER THE EARTHQUAKE WAS COLD, DISMAL, disheartening. Long periods of rain, a snowfall that actually covered the ground for two weeks, a lot of mud, a seeming never end to hunger, a lot of sickness, a mortality rate that was staggering.

The Bonners and Martinezes shared the house on Nineteenth Street for six months. Then the Martinezes left to join Alex's brother, Enrique, and his family in a larger house that had more space and two fireplaces.

During the six months the two families shared the house on Nineteenth, James and Alex were able to install windows which cut down on drafts that brought cold air inside during the darkest months of winter.

Lori and Alex's wife Rita worked together in the kitchen and became very creative in creating tasty meals out of random ingredients available. About once a month the adults shared a bottle of cheap wine when it reappeared in local groceries which often featured only large numbers of empty shelves.

The two men also located an old wood-burning stove and installed it in the fireplace in the Nineteenth Street house. They fired up the stove in early December, guaranteeing warmth in at least the living room, with a little of the heat escaping to adjoining rooms and upstairs bedrooms. Otherwise they were like igloos.

Trees around Forest Grove came down one by one as the community's need for firewood rose exponentially. The trees were split with chainsaws and then dissected further with axes, hatchets and handsaws.

In February, a glimmer of normalcy returned to Forest Grove when the city's water department obtained enough diesel fuel to resume operation of the city's water purification plant. This brought to an end the necessity of boiling water before it could be swallowed safely.

James and Alex obtained enough work to bring a modest flow of cash into their homes. Much of their work involved emergency repairs to roofs and outside walls after high winds in December caused extensive damage throughout the Willamette Valley.

For Lisa, managing a toddler and a baby under 1850s' conditions was a constant struggle. Keeping Lori and her infant brother warm undergirded every activity she undertook during the long winter. Initially water used for cooking and washing had to be brought home in jugs hauled in a wheelbarrow. This chore mercifully ended when the water purification plant resumed operating.

Restoration of water pressure also brought back functioning toilets, which the two families welcomed. It ended trips day and night to the outhouse in the back yard.

The cruelest part of that long winter for Lisa was not having electricity available. She fondly recalled washing Lori's diapers in a washing machine before the earthquake. Washing diapers by hand after boiling water on a stove was an unwelcome chore. Disposables were nowhere to be found.

Kerosene that could be used to provide light after dark was almost impossible to find, so the Bonners and Martinezes retired shortly after sundown. As winter gave way to spring and the days grew longer with each passing week, hopes also grew along with more hours of daylight.

When February came, James dug up half the grass area in the backyard and he and Lisa planted a garden, following instructions in a booklet they found in the library. In April the town's micro brewery reopened, which brought cheer to local residents. Since neither James nor Lisa had much desire for alcohol, they skipped the initial celebration, but did join the crowds at an annual spring festival sponsored by the brewery, the saki distillery and local merchants along Main and Pacific streets.

The Bonners' garden did well at the outset, except for strawberries. That early crop, which appeared in May, vanished after browsing deer from the woods west of town discovered it. Anticipating more deer visits, James scoured the area for some wire fencing and built a wall around the garden to discourage the local Bambis. It worked and the Bonners were rewarded with beans, asparagus and other vegetables as summer brought warmer temperatures.

Along the way the family stumbled across an old scale—no batteries required—and Lisa started keeping records of the family members' weights. Some initial concerns about Skip not gaining weight worried Lisa, who saw he was not putting on pounds, but that was offset by his activity level which was over the top.

The siblings generally got along well until Skip discovered throwing Lori's small doll collection around like bean bags was fun. That game ended when one of the dolls collided with a kerosene lamp, knocking it to the floor, causing some of the kerosene to leak.

One of Lisa's continuing challenges was finding toilet paper to buy. She became friends with two nearby market owners who would tip her off when a small shipment arrived at the back door. The Bonners never ran out, but came very close on several occasions including one time when person(s) unknown raided their outhouse and took away the end of a roll. After that, toilet paper was kept in the house, making a trip to the outhouse only when it was needed and then returned to the house for safekeeping. The task was simplified when Forest Grove's sewage treatment plant resumed operation.

The condom crisis came to an end when both James and Lisa found packets for sale at different locations on the same day and each brought their finds home. Sex resumed, which was very welcome.

A plus side of the long period before electricity was restored was a sharp increase in neighbor-to-neighbor contact. Next-door visits over the fence became common and children were able to roam from their front yards with parents' knowledge that neighbors also at home would be keeping watch over them.

Other plusses appeared as the first year following the earthquake ended and another began. On long summer evenings Lisa and James would sit on the front porch, talking quietly, waving to neighbors as they strolled by.

After Skip grew older and learned to walk, he and Lori started playing a rude form of badminton using Ping-Pong paddles instead of badminton racquets. When a battered shuttlecock was hit into the street, the kids would stop and stare at the porch. James would get out of his chair and retrieve the shuttlecock and the game would resume.

Eventually James built a taller makeshift "net" out of surplus clothesline and two broom handles, sharpened at the end to anchor them in the ground. One of the brooms had been broken earlier in its life, so James reassembled it with the aid of duct tape. Ugly, but it got the job done. Old rags attached to the clothesline added an artistic touch while reducing kids colliding with the net.

Work opportunities for James and Alex Martinez kept increasing and after a year they found they were working five days a week and occasionally six. Gradually more money found its way to their savings account in the Forest Grove State Bank, a small institution that had avoided being swept up in mergers. Both Lisa and James knew Herbert Watkins, the bank's owner and manager. He was very cautious with money—his own included—and they felt safe with him in charge. Their interest the first year after the quake earned them $1.72 in US dollars.

Chapter 6

Anarchy, Rise of the Malvadoes

ANARCHY CAME TO THE EARTHQUAKE-BATTERED NORTHWEST IN different ways and timelines. At the outset, looting ended quickly as thieves discovered the lack of electricity made big-screen TVs, smart phone games and cell phones useless. A sudden loss of cell phones crippled all communications, the impact felt by every individual, business and government agency.

For those needing emergency help in a hurry, loss of 911 service became the new reality since the alternative was to walk or bicycle to a police or fire station. If no officer was in the police station, help came glacially or not at all. If someone was there, they contacted the nearest police officer by a 20-year-old-plus radio system rescued from a long-neglected storage room.

Gardens offered a low-tech crime target. James, like many of his neighbors, spent many nights in summer listening for an unusual sound that told him someone, most likely a teenager, was trying to reach through his fence to grab some strawberries or other edibles.

Serious crimes spiked once the first trickle of gasoline reappeared in the area, the most notable being a bank robbery in nearby Hillsboro.

In the second spring after the quake a new threat arrived in the Willamette Valley. A motorcycle gang with 30 members or so started attacking small, remote rural high schools. Somehow the gang acquired high-powered weapons that enabled them to overwhelm small-town police departments or county sheriff's deputies who responded. The officers were hopelessly outnumbered and outgunned when they attempted to stop the gang. A number of deputies paid the ultimate price—loss of their lives.

A Hispanic community in Lane County coined the name "Malvadoes" for the gang, the word a loose translation of "the wicked ones."

Wicked turned out to be a gross understatement. The Malvadoes were brutal, perverted killers. Their plan of attack was to roar into school parking lots, now largely empty of cars and trucks, surround the school with armed guards and then storm inside. At gunpoint they forced students, teachers and school staffers to go to the school's gym or cafeteria.

Once gathered, the students were ordered to sit on bleachers if present. Then, after shooting out some overhead lamps in the ceiling to install more fear, they would order the most attractive girls and a few handsome boys to come down to the floor of the gym. Those chosen were roughly stripped, sodomized and raped in front of their horrified classmates. Woe to the 15-year-old sophomore girl whose breasts were fully developed. Even more woe to any teenager who resisted. At the second high school attacked by the Malvadoes, 16-year-old Phyllis Johnson greeted the soft penis thrust into her mouth by biting down hard. The enraged Malvadoe withdrew his appendage and hit Phyllis's jaw with enough force to break it. He then ripped off the last of her clothes, bit her nipples savagely and raped her. His syphilis provided ongoing suffering.

Any resistance brought a deadly response. Occasionally a Malvadoe would fire into the bleachers setting off more screams and panic as the traumatized students hunkered down seeking safety where no safety existed. Teachers who protested were executed on the spot. Students who tried to escape to seek help were gunned outside the school if they reached an outside door.

If a cell phone call brought a response from a local law enforcer and a sheriff's car approached the school, it was raked by fire from AK-47s held by Malvadoes stationed as sentries. Shots riddled the vehicle and brought quick death to the one or two deputies inside.

After the Malvadoes' second attack, sheriffs from five counties met in Brownsville to craft a response to the Malvadoes menace. They quickly decided to ask the state and federal governments for help and contacted the governor's office asking for a meeting.

Governor Angela Beckwith-Schall, latest in a string of liberal Portlanders to hold the governor's office for the state's ruling party, met with the sheriffs. She pledged support in dealing with the gang but offered no specific commitments.

The law officers left the meeting wondering what, if anything, they had achieved. Beckwith-Schall seemed detached, her mind focused suggested possible ways the state could take to stop the Malvadoes' rampage.

They were right. Falling state revenues were colliding with demands for more post earthquake help. Compounding the state's fiscal woes was the skyrocketing costs of the state's billions of dollars upside down public employee pension fund.

Public employee unions were Beckwith-Schall's political base. They and their members were feeling the impact of shrinking income tax collections and she had to keep their leaders happy if she wanted a second term as governor.

The Oregon National Guard and State Police were both handicapped by loss revenues, both state and federal. The Guard had tightened security at armories and weapons depots around the state. Crime investigators from the State Police had begun assembling a detailed report on the Malvadoes. Multiple witnesses had been interviewed.

All the law enforcement investigators were handicapped by lack of information about the Malvadoes. Where were they headquartered? How did they obtain the gasoline for their motorcycles? How did they manage to appear from nowhere and vanish after their raids?

The law agencies appealed to recreational drone owners who readily volunteered to help monitor rural areas, but coverage was patchy and they never spotted the Malvadoes before the gang struck. Shortages of batteries and power interruptions also hampered deployment of the drone "force," but it gradually improved its surveillance.

The Guard and State Police established a command headquarters in Albany and helicopters were deployed to Salem, Corvallis, Eugene and Aurora.

Meanwhile additional Malvadoes attacks followed, one in rural Clackamas County, the other in Polk County south of Dallas. The latter drew a National Guard unit from Salem that ended in disaster. As the Malvadoes emptied the smashed high school and roared away on their motorcycles they stopped at the crest of a hill, turned and hit the military convoy with streams of bullets from AK-47s which proved lethal. One of the attackers was struck when the surprised Guardsmen returned fire. Unfortunately, he died before he could be interviewed, so no useful information was obtained.

Two weeks later the Malvadoes struck a newly opened Christian high school, Wynwood Academy, in western Yamhill County. One of the students ordered from the bleachers in the school gym was Joseph Lipinski, a 17-year-old who spent five hours a day six days a week in a McMinnville gym building his body into a godlike form. With a chest almost twice the size of his waist and heavily muscled arms, he was attacked by four homosexual Malvadoes who had to struggle to flatten him on the gym floor and keep him there.

Tearing off his clothes, all four Malvadoes raped him face down as their cohorts used their collective 650 pounds to keep him pinned to the floor.

The fourth Malvadoe to rape Joseph, Butch Tomas, then reached beneath the youth, grabbed his testicles and castrated him.

Joseph's scream cut through the noise of the room as his blood flowed onto the gym floor. Butch then popped Joseph's balls into his mouth and sucked out the two orbs. Hurling the empty scrotum sack aside, he turned to his stunned companions, grinned and said, "Rocky Mountain oysters, best I ever had."

A week later a conversation over lunch changed James Bonner's life forever. He, Alex and Herb Grindahl, a plumber, were renovating part of a barn into a residence several miles south of Forest Grove off Oregon Highway 47. Their topic soon centered on the Malvadoes.

Was Forest Grove High School or more likely smaller Gaston High at risk? What could be done to halt the Malvadoes' rampage, a topic that had the general public, at least outside Portland, moving from fear to panic?

"Maybe it's time to think outside the box," James offered as he wolfed down a cheese sandwich Lisa had prepared. "I was approached last night by friends who feel something drastic has to happen to stop the Malvadoes menace. But so far no one has come up with an idea to make this happen."

The next day when James and Alex hoped to finish the pole barn project they were joined by Betsy Nobles, an electrician who also was completing a rewiring of the barn. Conversation about the Malvadoes resumed.

"We really know little about the Malvadoes," Alex observed. "They number 30 or so. They hit small remote high schools. Their attacks last 45 minutes to an hour and then they vanish."

"They target young people, teenagers, and they like good-looking ones," Betsy pointed out.

"What if," she paused, "what if someone or some group set up a trap for the Malvadoes. Maybe a late summer graduation party or concert sort of like Vortex gathering back in the 1970s?

"You remember the story. Governor Tom McCall wanted to avoid anti-Vietnam protesters from clashing with American Legionnaires holding their annual convention in Portland. He was talked into a plan to keep the Legionnaires and anti-Vietnam War protesters apart by sponsoring a rock festival at MacIver State Park on the

Clackamas River, all financed by McCall's Republican friends. The State Police shielded the event with all its alcohol, drugs and nudity from local Rednecks. McCall thought his political career was finished but Vortex turned out to be a stroke of genius.

"Downtown Portland did not become a war zone. McCall even got reelected."

"This idea has merit," James said. "Lure the Malvadoes into a trap. Advertise the party, maybe as sort of a super high school graduation party. Find a location that can be sealed off."

"So, if the Malvadoes take the bait and show up, what happens next?" Alex asked.

"This is where this conversation goes deep secret. I mean totally secret," James said.

"Excuse me, but this is where I bow out," Betsy said. "I don't want to be anywhere near the Malvadoes no matter what is planned."

"Sure Betsy," Herb replied. "Talk about the party is fine. Total silence otherwise on the Malvadoes."

"Agreed," she said. "If you want, I'll talk to the IBEA about financial support for the party, for food and refreshments—nonalcoholic, I presume—to keep the campers happy.

After both she and Herb left, James turned to Alex.

"Alex, we're talking ambush. We wipe them out. All of them. No more rampage."

The next day James, Alex and Alex's older brother, Jorge, met at Jorge's house. No one else was present. The meeting was brief. They agreed on three preliminary tasks. One was to obtain the latest detailed maps of the Coast Range. Second was lining up some heavy equipment to clean up the site where the Malvadoes would be attacked. Third and most important was identifying good marksmen who would maintain secrecy about the plot up to the moment it would occur.

Chapter 7

Sponge Meadows

IT TOOK MULTIPLE TRIPS, BUT THE TRIO FINALLY FOUND WHAT they felt was a good spot to confront the Malvadoes. It was a largely abandoned logging road, narrow, flanked by two ditches filled with stagnant water. On the north side of the road a two-story, steeply sloping wall was topped by a forest on the ridge. The south side was more level, a replanted forest with little underbrush.

Jorge ,who had served with the Army's Special Forces in two deployments in Afghanistan, proved to be a valuable asset at this point.

Examining the site he told them it was perfect for an ambush. The logging road had been stabilized by bringing infill to bolster the soft mud that it ran across. The name, Sponge Meadows, described it perfectly, Jorge felt.

The road itself continued west to the Coast Range crest where a church youth camp had operated for decades before declining youth participation in church had caused it to close. The main route to and from the camp ran west toward the Wilson River Highway and was flanked by scattered homes and carried a fair amount of traffic.

That would encourage the Malvadoes to favor the Sponge Meadows approach, Jorge felt.

Jorge cautioned the planners. Whoever joined them in this exercise had to be careful to keep their fire aimed squarely on the road. Anyone who shot above the road stood a good chance of killing one of the ambushers across the road, he told James, Alex and Herb.

Planning went forward. New recruits were added, all having recognized skills in handling firearms and understanding they would face a major challenge. They pledged to keep total silence about "the project."

As days and weeks west by leading up to the "graduation campout" party, leadership of the effort centered more and more on James Bonner who had never been chosen to lead before. Always calm, he proved able to reach a decision after learning as many facts as possible and remained totally focused on the goal of restoring peace and calm to the Willamette Valley by destroying the Malvadoes.

James did not seek leadership. He just provided it and those around him came to trust him when a serious topic came up.

Those joining the project ventured into the forests for target practice and under James's leadership evolved into three groups, one to occupy the ridge line on one side of the road, the second cadre to occupy the level opposite side.

The third group with only four members would be stationed in a collapsing shack a mile back down their escape route. The third group's mission was to notify the main group the Malvadoers were coming and to ensure no Malvadoe escaped to report the planned wipe-out. Again, secrecy, secrecy, secrecy.

Amazingly, secrecy was maintained right up to the point the graduating high schoolers gathered for their campout in mid-August. More than 300 came bringing their sleeping bags, tents and camping gear. Betsy Noble came through with a nice donation from the IBEW which purchased food and nonalcoholic drinks. The union's contribution was matched by three banks. Together they provided enough money to finance a band. The party was on.

Betsy also contacted three sheriff's departments and convinced them to provide a security ring around the campground for the entire weekend of the party. She said nothing about the effort to confront the Malvadoes while encouraging the lawmen to use the road leading west toward the coast. The lawmen would block any party crashers and the just curious away from the partying teens.

It all came together. The weather was perfect.

One question remained. Would the Malvadoes take the bait? At 11:30 a.m. on Saturday, the Bonner group had their answer. The guard shack radioed a warning. Four minutes later the main force heard the sound of motorcycles coming up the road.

Then they appeared, strung out over 200 yards as the last of the column came into view. With all the Malvadoes in view Jorge Martinez drew a bead on the lead motorcyclist and fired his M4. Two other shots from the ridge followed. All three hit their target and the lead Malvadoes cycle crashed into the water on the lower side of the road. The driver, flung from the machine, floated face down in the muck, blood flowing from his neck and back.

The forest erupted in gunfire. The carnage was instantaneous. One Malvadoe raised an AK-47 to return fire, but a rain of bullets slammed into him and the weapon fell to the dirt road unused. Within five minutes all of the Malvadoes were dead or dying, some falling under motorcycles as they spun out of control. Others fell on their sides or slid into ditches.

Three of the Malvadoes managed to cross the ditches and seek safety in the woods, but they were fully visible from the top of the ridge. None reached the woods alive.

The firing ceased when all of the Malvadoes stopped moving. Silence returned as the marksmen in the woods and on top of the ridge made their way into the open and met on the body-strewn dirt track. Only one of the ambushers was hurt. He scraped his leg when he slipped on a loose rock coming down from the ridge.

Under James's direction the dead bodies were placed on a thrown-together travois and dragged through the woods to two long trenches that had been dug in advance. Wallets, money and identifying rings and earrings were removed and placed in large black plastic bags which were dropped in the trenches along with the bodies. The victors were following orders issued earlier: no souvenirs, all evidence buried.

Others rolled the motorcycles, most of them big Harleys or similar-size machines, farther down the road and into a clearing where two other ditches had been dug earlier. Gasoline was siphoned off into cans before the machines were rolled into the ditches. When all the machines and bodies were in the ditches, dirt and weeds were thrown on top of the pits to cover them completely. Additional brush was brought from the surrounding area and carefully placed on the new mounds.

We'll have to keep checking on this area, James thought. Meanwhile the last of the volunteers rolled a horse-drawn water tank down the road, mixing bloodstained dirt and gravel in an effort to flush away evidence. Ditches on both sides of the road were given a final inspection to make sure nothing had been overlooked.

Finally, when the work had been completed, James called the group together for a debriefing. He thanked them for their hard work and risking their lives and reminded them that the longer the ambush remained a secret, the safer each one of them and their families were.

"We hope this is the final chapter of the Malvadoes, but we're not sure. If there are others out there, they will want revenge and they will be looking for each one of us. We'll be targets. Our families will be targets.

"So we'll keep listening for reports of another Malvadoes attack. Hopefully they won't resume once schools reopen in this fall.

"Let's stay in touch, just in case a threat surfaces and we have to get together quickly. I'm passing a clipboard around. I'd appreciate each of you listing the best way to contact you just in case it's necessary.

"Thank you again for what you did today. It wasn't pretty. It was necessary to solve a crisis that otherwise was not being solved. We hope and pray it worked."

* * *

Four miles away, backed into a copse of firs alongside another dirt road, an unmarked 53-foot-long trailer and its tractor remained parked. In its cab 57-year-old Bobby "Nails" Towns slept. When he awoke, around 5 p.m. he was astounded when he looked at his watch and saw the time.

"Where are my motorcyclists," he wondered. They were long overdue. Bobby worried. This had not happened before. Each of their attacks had lasted no longer than three hours in the past. This time four hours had passed and there was no sign of the gang. No phone call came explaining a delay. He opened a thermos of coffee, drank its final contents and turned on a radio at a very low volume.

At six p.m. Bobby made a call on his cell phone, something he had been told repeatedly never to do in the past. No one answered. Now bordering on panic, he turned on the diesel motor and let its engine warm up. Twenty-five minutes later he put the truck into low gear and the rig inched its way forward on to the road.

Bobby switched on his lights and started driving, first on a gravel road, then on a paved two-lane paved county road. When he reached Interstate 5, he rounded the curve and started north toward Portland. An hour later he got off I-5 at the Columbia Boulevard interchange and turned east toward the industrial warehouse area three miles away.

Once there, he made a sharp turn into a wide driveway, pulled forward another 100 yards and circled around a two-story warehouse to the north side. Then he pressed a button and watched a large metal door scroll its way up its rails far enough that he could run the entire tractor and 53-foot trailer inside. He then lowered the warehouse door which hit the concrete slab with a bang.

Bobby turned off the truck's engine, climbed down from the cab and walked a few yards to a battered 20-year-old pickup. Climbing inside, he drove the pickup to the south side of the warehouse and opened a smaller overhead door. He drove his small truck outside the building and again lowered the overhead door.

He reached for his cell phone. It was Saturday and he wanted to meet his long-time friend Gonzo for some beers, their usual Saturday routine. He never got passed the area code. A sudden pain hit Bobby's chest. He collapsed in the front seat of the truck. The heart attack came out of nowhere, but it was fatal.

Years later the warehouse's owner returned home after working most of his adult life in Abu Dhabi. The warehouse was one of a string of aging industrial properties he had inherited in North America. He had ongoing trouble renting it and had finally found a client who offered him a minimum sum per month. He had accepted the offer, had asked few questions and had not been surprised when the rental payments stopped abruptly. His attention was focused elsewhere where he was earning huge sums and he rarely thought about the warehouse.

Returning to Portland when he retired, he eventually checked on the warehouse, found a tractor trailer inside and was surprised to discover two ranks of sleeping bunks, tattered blankets and old sleeping bags inside. The lower bunks surprisingly were five feet above the trailer's floor which contained small tracings of motor oil. The truck and trailer's license plates were years out of date. Papers inside the cab listed a corporate office and address which turned out to be bogus.

The owner then contacted the Oregon Public Utilities office. After three months he received authorization to remove the vehicle and sell it. The motorcycle gang's connection to the truck remains undetected to this day.

Chapter 8

Secret No More

Sponge Meadows remained a secret for exactly 12 days. The silence was broken in the back room of a small bar in Cornelius when an off-duty sheriff's detective, Bob Henderson, decided to try a hand or two of video poker on a night when the lights were on in the community. That was infrequent and never lasted long.

The video poker was not going well and he was ready to quit and go home when he overheard a man sitting nearby say the Malvadoes wouldn't be rampaging anymore.

He immediately turned around and spotted the man, an empty beer stein in front of him, repeat what he had just said.

Reaching the booth Henderson introduced himself, but not his job title, and offered to buy a round of beer for the three men seated in the booth.

"What you say about the Malvadoes is great news. What makes you say it?" he asked, taking a seat.

The talker, age 22, hesitated for a moment, but regained his confidence as the waitress deposited another pitcher in front of the group.

"Let's just say they ran into a problem in the Coast Range weekend before last."

"A problem?"

"Like an ambush. They got wiped out, all of them."

"How do you know this? Did someone tell you?" Henderson asked quietly.

"I was there. It was like a shooting gallery except for dead bodies and wrecked motorcycles all over the road."

"No shit," the man on the talker's right said before raising his glass of beer again.

"So how many of you were there taking on the Malvadoes?" Henderson asked, trying to be a mere curiosity seeker.

"I don't know. Twenty, maybe 25."

"It sounds like it was planned. Who organized it?" Henderson asked.

"James Bonner. I really don't know him. He's a quiet guy. He builds houses, I believe."

Soon after that, the sheriff's detective left the group. Reaching his car, he called the sheriff.

* * *

At 6:30 a.m. an unmarked sheriff's car pulled up in front of James and Lisa's house on Nineteenth. Dressed casually in a blue sweater and black slacks, Detective Bob Henderson walked up to the front door and rang the bell.

James answered it.

"Are you James Bonner?"

"I am and you are?"

"Bob Henderson, senior detective, Washington County Sheriff's Department."

"Come on in. Could you use a cup of coffee? Lisa, we have a visitor. Can you bring us some coffee? Cream or sugar?" he asked Henderson.

Surprised by the reception he did not expect, Henderson stepped into the living room and closed the door behind him.

"Have a seat," James said. "I believe I know why you are here. It's a little early for a social call."

Lisa, still in her night robe, brought coffee, smiled at Henderson and then withdrew to the kitchen after James introduced him.

Henderson recounted the previous night's conversation. "Is it true, the Malvadoes were wiped out?"

"Yes they were," James replied, looking Henderson straight in the eye as he spoke.

"You organized this?"

"I'll take responsibility. Someone had to take action and I didn't see any real signs that anyone in power was doing anything about it except for the sheriff's deputies who died while trying to defend high school students who didn't deserve to be raped and killed."

James put his coffee mug down.

"I have a question. What happens next?"

Henderson drew a deep breath.

"Normally, I file a report. The sheriff reviews it and turns evidence over to the district attorney who submits it to a grand jury. The grand jury decides to indict or not indict.

"Bonner, let's be frank. This is no ordinary case. The deaths of 30 or more men can't be ignored. On the other hand, the Malvadoes were no saints. Every high schooler's parents in western Oregon has you to thank for what you did. If the Malvadoes are no more, it's a blessing. And putting you in prison for the rest of your life will strike these folks as a worse crime than a mass murder of terrorizing thugs.

"All I can tell you now is don't leave the State of Oregon. I will give my report to the sheriff. He will start the legal machinery and that likely will require your arrest and detention. The District Attorney will want to talk to you, I'm sure.

"The real question is how far does the DA want to go on this matter. So far all we have is two statements, but no other evidence."

"Well, thank you for not taking me away in handcuffs today. I'm remodeling a bathroom in a home up on the heights if you need me.

Also, here's my cell phone number if you call when we have electricity available." He handed Henderson a business card.

Henderson took the card.

"By the way, Bonner, how old are you?"

"Twenty-six."

* * *

Veteran Washington County District Attorney Ken Matthewson knew he was holding an activated bomb the minute Henderson's report hit his desk. A monstrous crime, a voluntary confession, the accused a hero who had eliminated a crime wave which him a hero to every parent in the Willamette Valley.

Matthewson also knew there were no bodies, no crime scene located and identified and no witnesses readily available to testify against Bonner. Then a possible escape hatch appeared in his mind. The massacre Bonner confessed to occurred in the Coast Range, but was it east or west of the Washington-Tillamook County Line?

He sent Henderson back to Bonner. The answer he got was not the one he wanted. The county line ran through Sponge Meadows, but precisely where would be hard to determine. The border had been surveyed many years ago. Matthewson decided he should contact his Tillamook County counterpart, Peter Clough, a very young and largely inexperienced prosecutor.

He telephoned Clough. They agreed to meet at the Forestry Exhibit Center on the Wilson River Highway the next day. Mathewson suggested Clough bring Tillamook County Sheriff Todd Richardson with him. Matthewson also invited Norm Hatch, Washington County's sheriff. Hatch could not come but sent Washington County Undersheriff Olivia Nelson in his place.

When the foursome sat down at a table in a quiet corner in the back of the exhibit hall, Matthewson laid out the Bonner/Malvadoes/Sponge Meadows scenario.

Clough's initial reaction did not surprise Matthewson. "Why is

41

Bonner not in custody? A crime this monstrous, the deaths of 30 or more men. This requires the full punishment of the law. Tillamook County will prosecute this case and seek Bonner's conviction. Anarchy of this type has to be dealt with forcefully and Tillamook County will do it."

What Clough missed in making this little speech was the facial reaction of his sheriff. Richardson immediately recognized the public relations disaster that loomed on the horizon. Finally, he spoke.

"Clough, do you want to be a one-term DA? If this matter goes to trial, do you think a jury would convict a man who met real anarchy head on after the State of Oregon repeatedly failed in its core mission of protecting the public? How many mothers and fathers of slain and raped teenagers do you want blocking the street in front of your house day after day shouting their outrage?"

"Richardson has spelled out the problem perfectly," Matthewson said. "How can you get a conviction when no one wants to testify against the accused? This case would be a defense attorney's dream come true, witness after witness spelling out the Malvadoes criminal actions against their children."

The picture came into focus for Clough. A jury finding Bonner not guilty, a humiliation for a prosecutor. The one-term DA concept suddenly made total sense.

"What do you suggest?" he asked Matthewson.

"I would suggest we issue a joint statement saying lack of evidence makes prosecution of James Bonner unwise at this time. We will ask the sheriffs of our counties to examine the Sponge Meadows area for evidence. They will report back that they found no evidence indicating a mass shooting. So we, the two district attorneys, will not seek an indictment. Taxpayer money will not be wasted."

* * *

When word of the two district attorneys' decision reached the State Capitol, reaction was swift. Governor Angela Beckworth-Schall immediately summoned Attorney General Ivan Beretsky to her office.

"This is unbelievable," Beckworth-Schall declared. "This man, James Bonner, is responsible for the deaths of 30 men. He confessed to it. He should be tried, convicted and spend the rest of his life in prison.

"I want action. I want it now. So tell me what you can do to insure the laws of Oregon apply to this mass murderer?"

"This is a new field for me," Beretsky replied. "I will examine the law, but I believe the first step is for you, the governor, to be ready to declare martial law in Washington and Tillamook counties and then send in the State Police and/or the National Guard to arrest Bonner. While we are working on the details, let's keep this secret."

"One more thing," Beckwith-Schall said. "When Bonner is arrested, have him taken to the Multnomah County jail. I don't trust Hillsboro to keep him confined and I know we can find Multnomah County jurors that won't turn him loose."

Unfortunately for Beckwith-Schall and Beretsky, the secrecy part of their planning died instantaneously. Unbeknown to them, Benicia Agustin was emptying wastebaskets in an adjoining office and heard the governor and attorney general's conversation in full. She hurried away as soon as she was able and phoned her brother, Roberto, and told him what she had heard.

Benicia felt very differently about James Bonner. Her youngest brother, Umberto, 16, had been raped by two homosexual Malvadoes when they stormed his high school in rural Benton County. This took place in full view of the student body assembled and cowering on the gym's bleachers and facing AK-47s pointed at them.

When the Malvadoes left after firing several shots into the bleachers, Umberto's girlfriend Carmelita Lopez and a neighbor, Eric Jones, rushed to help Umberto pull his clothes back on.

If James Bonner really wiped out the Malvadoes, he was a hero. He did not deserve to spend the rest of his life in prison, Benicia felt.

She was not alone. By grapevine, 40 minutes later, word of the pending arrest reached Bonner and Alex Martinez while they were adding a deck to a house in north Forest Grove.

"You must hide," their informant said.

"I'm not going to hide," James replied. "I gave my word I would stay in Forest Grove and be available if they needed me.

"Thank you for bringing me this latest development," he added. "There are some details I have to take care of if I'm going to be arrested."

His most important assignment was telling Lisa, Lori and Skip of what lay ahead. Somehow James felt this episode would have a good outcome even though at this point he could not think of a possible scenario with that result.

Two mornings later, four helicopters dropped down into Rogers Park. Forty soldiers in full combat gear jumped out and starting walking in two files, rifles in hand, to the Bonner home three blocks away. Simultaneously, National Guard jeeps pulled up in front of Forest Grove's city hall and police station. Martial law posters went up and local police were told they now operated under martial law requirements.

At the Bonner home, James and the family waited until the doorbell rang and a lieutenant informed James he was under arrest.

James kissed Lisa, hugged Lori and Skip, and then accompanied the lieutenant to the curb where a 3/4-ton military truck waited. By the time they climbed into the vehicle, neighbors had started to gather, clearly upset at what they were witnessing. The small crowd swelled to 100 as the soldiers arrived at the scene on a run and then turned around and escorted the vehicle and Bonner back to the waiting choppers.

As the vehicle left the scene, James raised his hands, now handcuffed, and gave the crowd a thumbs up. The neighbors remained silent and turned their backs on the soldiers as the procession disappeared around a corner.

Inside the house, Lisa prayed.

Chapter 9

Ricochet

WHEN HE WAS BOOKED INTO MULTNOMAH COUNTY'S JUSTICE Center, James asked when he could expect to see a lawyer: The reply: Soon.

Ninety minutes later two jail deputies took him to a small conference room where he came face to face with Christopher Barnum. Barnum looked young, like he had just graduated from high school. He introduced himself as a new member of the Oregon Bar specializing in property and estate issues.

Barnum initiated the conversation by asking James if he had legal counsel or wanted to employ a lawyer to defend him against the charges he faced.

"I don't know any lawyers. I understand they are expensive," James replied.

Barnum agreed. A top-flight criminal lawyer would expect fees ranging from $50,000 on up, he said.

"I don't have that kind of money. So, you're stuck with my case?"

"Looks like it," Barnum said. The two men seated themselves on opposite sides of a small metal table.

"A question," James said. "If you specialize in property and estate issues, how did you wind up defending an accused mass murderer?"

Barnum looked him square in the eye. "You will be found guilty." He continued, "This case reeks of politics. The governor wants you found guilty and your case wound up in Multnomah County because Washington and Tillamook counties declined to prosecute. The governor and her ruling party predecessors appointed every judge in this courthouse including Presiding Judge Annabelle Oso, who is a very close personal friend of the governor. The two of them are confident this case will draw a jury panel that sees the world in the same way they do."

"Well, thanks for spelling it out in such clear terms," James replied. "How do you as my defense counsel plan to respond?"

"First of all I want to see material the prosecution puts together. Then I will contact the district attorneys of Washington and Tillamook counties. We will see who the prosecution plans to call to testify. We'll learn whether they plan to search the Sponge Meadows site for evidence. Then we'll decide who we want to call to testify.

"Bonner, this whole charade is on fast track. Don't be surprised if the trial starts next week. The timing will depend on when the prosecution feels it has what it needs to convict you.

"Also, you should not testify on grounds of potential self- incrimination, a privilege long observed in Oregon courts. And, can you provide me with a short list of people you know well today or have known in the past who can testify under oath that they have no link to your alleged crime?

"As for other witnesses I would like to put one or more persons on the stand who can describe firsthand their experiences with the Malvadoes. Their testimony could have a real impact on the jury.

"Lastly, the prosecutors feel totally certain you will be found guilty. Their overconfidence may cause them to stumble and make mistakes we can exploit. Even the best lawyers make mistakes once in a while. We can hope it happens.

"One final note. I know you would like to talk to your wife, but I hope that won't happen before the trial opens. If she comes to the jail or you talk over the phone, you may be sure every word said will be taped and turned over to the prosecution. I strongly advise she does not come here until the trial begins."

With that Barnum handed James his legal pad and a ballpoint pen.

"If you'd care to, write her a note. I'll make sure she receives it when I see her face to face, hopefully tomorrow."

* * *

THE TRIAL OPENED ONE WEEK LATER IN A COURTROOM IN THE new Multnomah courthouse room chosen for its limited seating for the public—benches that could seat 20 individuals comfortably.

Lisa Bonner arrived 45 minutes early escorted by a Washington County sheriff's deputy. She was denied entry because all seats in the courtroom were already taken. Christopher Barnum had anticipated this and told Lisa and the deputy to wait in the building's coffee shop while he attempted to talk to Judge Oso to ask if the accused's wife could replace one of the spectators already seated in the room.

Judge Oso said, "No." She added the same spectators would be given preference throughout the trial. Barnum countered by making sure young friends of his who worked at two local television stations learned of the judge's decision. After that, every report on the trial included word that the accused's wife had been barred from the courtroom. The decision did not sit well with many Oregonians, the numbers increasing each day the trial went forward.

"Mistake number one," Barnum told James as they took their seats at the defense counsel's desk on the opening day of the trial.

Jury panels in Oregon are drawn from a list of registered voters selected on a random basis. In this case, protocol was not followed fully. The pool was stacked with prospective jurors who were all known activists in the ruling party or spouses of activists in the party. Barnum exhausted his jury vetoes but did secure three jurors who had removed their names from the registered voters' lists but had drivers' licenses showing they were 18 or 19 years old. Thus they could qualify for jury service. At the end of the process, he felt perhaps two of the twelve chosen might judge Bonner fairly when the jury considered its verdict.

One of the first called to testify by the prosecution was Washington County Sheriff Norm Hatch.

They hit a stone wall. Hatch said he could not comment on the case before the court because the allegations remained under investigation triggered by actions taken by the governor, attorney general and Multnomah County authorities.

Judge Oso was not satisfied. Hatch did not budge. The case remained under investigation and he would not discuss it.

Oso ordered him testify. He refused. Oso brought her gavel down and declared Hatch was in contempt of court. She directed the bailiff to deliver the sheriff to the Justice Center Jail three blocks away.

Barnum leaned over to James and whispered, "Mistake No. 2."

The following day it was Barnum's opportunity to call witnesses. He entered into the record that James Bonner had never been arrested for a crime and had had a clean driving record since running a stop sign when he was 17 years old.

Two longtime friends testified that James Bonner was honest, a hard worker who had been his family's principal bread winner since he was a teenager, and that he was a good neighbor who helped those who needed help he could provide.

Barnum called his last witness, Alfreda Gonzales, an Albany resident thought to be related to the Malvadoes. Nothing they examined in the pretrial documents led the prosecutors to believe she might be a Malvadoes victim.

Bad error. After leading Alfreda through a number of background and personal history questions, Barnum asked the question he hoped would get the Malvadoes' record of carnage before the jurors.

"Living down in the Valley, do you know anyone who is connected to the Malvadoes?"

Judge Oso looked from the bench where she had been texting her husband about their evening plans and shot a look at the prosecutors' desk. She saw they too were momentarily distracted, long enough for Alfreda Gonzales' answer:

"I know the Malvadoes. They raped me and killed my brother Daniel when they attacked the Covenant Christian Academy last spring."

The chief prosecutor rose to his feet and asked Judge Oso to strike Alfreda Gonzales's statement from the record as non- germane to the case. "James Bonner is on trial here, not the Malvadoes whom he has confessed to killing," he said.

Oso ordered the jury to disregard her testimony.

"Mistake No. 3, huge," Barnum confided to James.

Barnum then stood and thanked Alfreda Gonzales for testifying. She left the courtroom but did not get by the media scrum guarding the exits from the building. Her comments led the news on TV, radio and newspapers and blogs over the next 24 hours.

The case went to the jury the following morning. It deliberated all day. It turned out three of the jurors had not followed Judge Oso's directive not to watch the case on television or discuss the case with outsiders. The jury was summoned back to the courtroom at 5 p.m. and then housed overnight in a downtown hotel where television had been cut from the rooms they slept in. They resumed their deliberations at 9 a.m. the following morning and at 1 p.m. sent word they had reached a verdict.

By this time the previously overconfident prosecutors were nervous because they had expected a short deliberation and quick verdict.

The jurors filed into the courtroom and took their seats, all except the foreman who turned out to be the panel's youngest member.

He opened a paper and read: "No bodies, no crime scene, no real evidence. The jury finds the defendant James Bonner not guilty."

Pandemonium erupted briefly in the courtroom before Judge Oso declared the matter closed and retreated to her chambers.

Two hours later, James hugged Lisa, Lori and Skip in their living room in Forest Grove. The family had a quiet dinner interrupted by neighbors who came to offer congratulations. The next morning James joined Alex Martinez at their latest work site, adding a room to a house in Gaston.

Chapter 10

"No" to "Yes"

"No. Absolutely not."

That was James's response when asked if he would ever be open to the idea that he become a candidate for governor of Oregon. He meant it. The tone of his voice made that clear.

The request came to him three days after he and Alex resumed work on adding a room to an old house in Gaston.

It began when a late model Cadillac Escalade drove up and parked in front of the house and two men, middle aged and attired in dark suits matching the elegance of the car, emerged.

Approaching the house they walked up a temporary ramp to the front porch and rang the bell. Alex answered it and asked them what they wanted. "James Bonner" was the reply. "Is he here?"

"He is, but he's busy. We're finishing up for the day. We need to clean up first."

"No problem. We'll wait in the car," the older of the duo said.

Twenty minutes later, James and Alex joined the two men in front of the house. The visitors introduced themselves: Jim Paterson, executive director of Oregon Businesses United and Noah Simpson, field director for Oregon Agribusiness, an umbrella group and political action arm of six statewide organizations.

James smiled. "Basically you are lobbyists," he said.

"Guilty as charged and we are here on business," Simpson, the younger of the two men replied.

"We're not buying," Alex volunteered. "We're short of cash and we probably don't need what you're selling."

"This is a sales call, but we're not after money," Simpson said.

"So what do you want?" James asked.

"We want you to run for governor and we have the resources to get you elected," Paterson said.

James laughed. So did Alex.

James's smile evaporated. "No way. Absolutely not. I've just had more public life than I ever wanted. I don't need more. I just want to be left alone. Besides," he recalled, "the primaries were weeks ago."

"You're right. The Democrats and Republicans have chosen their candidates. We want you to run as an independent.

"Bonner, take a look at this," Paterson said, pulling a document from his briefcase. "This is a survey, a poll of likely Oregon voters taken a week ago. The firm conducting it has a great track record. Turn to page 2, the highlighted section."

James flipped the page and read: Beckwith-Schall, Democrat, 38%; John Newton, Republican, 22%; James Bonner, Independent 30%.

"The breakdown shows you leading in the Willamette Valley outside Salem, Eugene and Corvallis. You are running even with Newton in southern Oregon and east of the Cascades. And that's with you not even being a candidate.

"You have name recognition and a strong potential base of support from people who appreciate the Malvadoes being eliminated, whatever the circumstances. They also know the Beckwith-Schall tried to put you behind bars for life. This poll shows they resent her and they're fired up.

"Bonner, the Democrats have held the governorship for three

generations. They are the ruling party. They have controlled the legislature and have held every statewide office for decades. Those outside the power structure see you as a way to turn Oregon around and reclaim the state from the hands of Portland liberal groupthink."

"Gentlemen, I'm not interested. I want to build homes. The last job I want is to be governor." James said "I want to enjoy my family. And if I did take you up on your offer, which I have no intention of doing, I would want no strings attached."

"That's the beauty of your candidacy, James," Noah Simpson offered. "You bring a fresh face to Oregon politics. You are a registered non-aligned voter with a reputation of being a hard worker and a leader willing to risk taking on a murderous gang of criminals.

"And frankly, the idea you want no strings attached is one our organizations can live with. We'll take the risk," Paterson said.

Paterson spelled out specifics of a campaign. "The only practical way at this point to getting on the November ballot is putting on a nominating convention that draws a minimum of 1,000 voters to a specific location at a specific time who are willing to sign a petition for your candidacy.

"My clients and Noah's clients feel that would be no real problem given the polling reports we just showed you.

"Actually I believe holding at least four separate nominating conventions would be a good idea—one in Clackamas County south of Portland, one in the lower Willamette Valley, possibly Albany, one in southern Oregon between Medford and Grants Pass and one east of the mountains either in Redmond or Hermiston."

"No thanks," James said. "I like my life as it is."

"Will you at least discuss it with your wife? You might tell her the salary is $140,000 per year and includes free housing if she doesn't mind living in the governor's mansion.

"One final note. The clock is running and the nominating conventions must be held no later than 20 days from now, so we will need a final answer from you no later than Thursday."

The two men handed James their calling cards. "I'll talk to Lisa. I'll give you an answer tomorrow," James said.

* * *

That evening Lisa and James retreated to the backyard after putting Lori and Skip to bed. The evening was pleasantly warm and it felt good to be outdoors.

James told Lisa about the lobbyists' visit that day and their request he run for governor as an Independent candidate.

"I don't like the idea at all," Lisa said. "I'm worried about what it could do to the children. I've been worried ever since the Malvadoes were crushed that someone, some group would want revenge and do something horrible to Lori and Skip. Every night I ask God to keep them and you safe."

"Sweetheart, I understand. I share your worry," James replied. "Besides that I am totally unprepared to be governor. I don't know what the governor does or how state government operates. My plate is already full dealing with unreliable electricity, the constant battle to get good tools and building materials, an old truck and the continuing struggle to find gasoline to run it. Besides, I ask myself, what good could I accomplish if I won the office?"

"James, I disagree with you on that point. I think you would surprise yourself. You are honest. You treat people fairly. People who know you trust you totally. If you did decide to run," Lisa continued, "I would insist on one condition. That's keeping the children out of public view. I don't want them involved in the campaign. I want them to have normal lives, not living under public scrutiny."

"If you did run and won the election, would we have to move to Salem, to a governor's mansion?"

"I don't think so," James countered. "It might be best if we did not move the family. I could either commute or spend a night or two a week in Salem. I'm not sure that's a great idea. I don't want to miss out on our kids' childhoods."

Five minutes of silence followed, each of them lost in their own thoughts.

Then, they heard "hello." A young man entered the backyard.

"Remember me, String Bean? I'm Don Lawson, the kid you rescued from three bullies when you were in fifth grade? I was in real trouble. You stood up to them. I went home in one piece."

James rose from his chair. The two men shook hands warmly, their left hands gripping the other's shoulder. James pulled up a third lawn chair for Don.

"Lisa, Don is the guy who carried me through the nightmare of Barbara Kinsolving my senior year. He coached me to a passing grade," James explained.

"So what brings you here tonight, Don? And, by the way, what's with the beard? I didn't recognize you."

"I'm a lobbyist. I work for Jim Paterson's firm. The beard makes me appear older, more mature," Don said. "I understand you were asked to run for governor today. I want you to know that I would like to work for you if you agree to do it.

"You would be king. I would be the Earl of Warwick, your right-hand man. You would make the decisions. My job would be to make sure you had the all the facts to base good decisions on. And if things go wrong, you can blame me.

"I really hope you run. I think you'd be great. You know, String Bean, I haven't seen you since high school. After I graduated, I picked up a political science degree at the University of Oregon. My entire time in Eugene I searched for a real conservative on the faculty. Never found one. The UO is a bastion of liberal-left 'groupthink.' So is the governor's office and the leadership of the boards and agencies she supervises.

"James, being in business with Alex Martinez, you live in the real world now reeling from the earthquake and the federal government's vanishing act. If you were governor, the whole state government would have a whole new perspective from the top.

"That's why I believe the state of Oregon would benefit by

having you in the governor's chair. If you go for it, I'd like to help you any way I can."

With that, Don rose from his chair. "I interrupted you two and I apologize. I'll be on my way."

"Don, before you go," Lisa said. "What's the story behind 'String Bean'?"

"Lisa, in grade school your husband was tall with long blond hair. He was thin, really thin. He looked like a string bean. At the same time, no one pushed him around. He just drew respect.

"Let me know what you two decide," Don concluded. He turned and left.

Looking at James now lost in thought, Lisa smiled. "You would like to do it, wouldn't you? Your friend Don is a great salesman."

"If I did agree to run, I might lose in November and our lives would go back to normal. But Simpson and Patterson would have to accept some conditions before I would agree to be a candidate."

"Such as?"

"Such as one term only. Then back to private life. During the campaign, you and the children are off limits. You will not be part of the campaign. Your life, their lives, stay private.

"I must have guaranteed time off to be a husband and father. Unless there is another earthquake, I'm governor five days a week max.

"During the campaign time, now to November, I campaign no more than two days a week so Alex and I fulfill commitments we have made.

"Last, but not least, I need a crash course in state government, its finances, the governor's responsibilities, powers and limits on those powers."

"Sounds reasonable to me. Make sure the gentlemen you talked to today understand you," Lisa concluded.

* * *

THOSE WHO URGED JAMES BONNER TO RUN FOR GOVERNOR accepted the terms he laid out immediately, knowing full well some likely would erode over time.

Efforts to convene the 1,000-voter nominating conventions hit high gear, resulting in five locations being chosen: Oregon City, Albany, Roseburg, Talent and Redmond.

The Bonners hosted a series of visitors who came to the house after dinner several times a week to give James a crash course on Oregon state government, its finances, and the powers and limitation on powers of the governor. Supervising it all was Don Lawson, who guided the discussions and acted as a reality check.

Don paid special attention to Lisa and made sure she was part of the discussion when topics touched on her or the children's lives. James quickly concluded he wanted Don's counsel on both the campaign and the governor's office should he be elected. Don immediately agreed to serve James in whatever capacity James wanted.

The five nominating conventions all drew well over the required 1,000 registered voters needed. Each meeting carefully followed the law to avoid legal challenges that might be forthcoming. Secretary of State Roberta Moon readily approved the Bonner candidacy, clearing the way for James to appear on the General Election ballot in November.

Under Don Lawson's guidance, James perfected a set speech—12 minutes long—in which he introduced himself and spelled out four major goals he wanted to accomplish in office: improve public schools, expand the State Police to deal with any Malvadoes threat in the future, restore reliable electric service statewide and rebuild Oregon's transportation infrastructure.

The remaining 45 minutes of each campaign stop called for James to take questions from the audience. If he didn't have an answer, he immediately acknowledged it and promised to provide an answer if the questioner would give him contact information.

Finally, it was agreed that Lisa, Lori and Skip would make only one appearance—on election night on the front porch of their home in Forest Grove.

Chapter 11

On to Fun City

James's first stop on the campaign trail was the Walmart parking lot in Canby. Even though the hour was early—8:30 a.m.—100 curious spectators had gathered around a temporary coffee stand on a clear September workday morning.

James and Don Lawson disembarked from the rented campaign car, a late model Toyota. James introduced himself and started slowly through the crowd. A middle-aged woman, probably a farm wife from her attire, offered him a cup of coffee, gushing effusively, "I'm so glad I had a chance to meet you." She handed James a blank sheet of paper and asked him to autograph it twice for her son and daughter. James handed her the coffee and scrawled "J Bonner" twice on the paper. Don meanwhile was supervising installation of a microphone on a portable stand placed on the bed of a farm truck. He signaled James it was time to start his talk. James climbed up to the platform, set the coffee aside, shuffled his notes and launched his campaign for governor by thanking those present for showing up. He then described why he was running for governor and what he hoped to accomplish in the office if he was elected.

Following Don Lawson's suggestions, he spoke slowly, frequently establishing eye contact with members of the audience. After finishing his prepared text, he set the speech papers down and invited questions.

The first two had been "planted" ahead of time. They were softball in nature, designed primarily to give members of his audience comfort in raising questions of their own.

The first question from the audience came from a man in a suit, possibly a lawyer. It invited James to tear into the incumbent governor's record.

James did not take the bait. Instead, he fell back on his theme of "this is what I will do or try to do" if elected.

A young girl, maybe 13, raised her hand. James recognized her and then asked, "Aren't you supposed to be in school?"

"I am in school," the girl replied. "I'm here on an assignment from my social studies teacher."

"Good for you. Good for your teacher. And, to be a better-informed voter, try to hear my opponents when they come to Canby. Now, your question."

The seventh grader noted her social studies class had 62 students in it. "What will you do to reduce that number if you think it should be reduced?"

"Sixty-two sounds like a lot to me, way too many if the teacher is doing more than just giving lectures and wants to make sure his or her students are learning more than memorizing facts.

Oregon is spending billions on K-12 education. More of that money should reach the classroom and not be diverted to other tasks in the field of education. He then cited administrative overhead and state contributions to retiree pension funds as two sources of money that possibly could be channeled into classrooms.

"Did I answer your question?" James asked the girl. She said she felt he had.

The question period passed swiftly. Signaled by Don that it was time to move on, James thanked the crowd again for coming and said he would appreciate their votes if they felt he was the best choice in the governor's race.

The Albany stop ran much the same way. Eugene was different.

The venue was Erb Memorial Union on the University of Oregon campus. Unlike Canby and Albany the crowd was not friendly. James was booed as he stepped to the microphone and the audience, almost all UO students, kept interrupting his talk. James decided to break away Don Lawson's script.

"Okay, folks, I have a question. Who is the oldest student here?" The hecklers suddenly went silent.

"I'm 26. Anyone here that age? Or older?"

"Hey, Macho. Raise your hand," someone in the back of the crowd yelled. The crowd responded: "Macho. We want Macho. A bearded 40-year-old-forever student, Macho found himself being pushed forward toward James and the podium.

"Come on up. Let's you and I have a little debate," James said.

Macho, bearded, scraggly hair, overweight from too many beers and two little exercise, lurched onto the platform and joined James behind the microphone. The crowd roared.

"Let's introduce ourselves, briefly," James said. "I'm James Bonner. I build and remodel homes. I have been the major bread-winner in my family since I was 16. I'm married. I have two children. I'm running for governor because 7,000 people attended nominating conventions last month. That qualified me for the November ballot."

As he handed the microphone to Macho, a question rang out. "How can you be governor if you never went to college?"

Macho hesitated and handed the microphone back toward James.

"No, no. You introduce yourself first," James insisted.

Macho turned to the crowd. "I'm Winton Stark. I'm a student at UO majoring in history, especially the lousy way we treat minorities in this country." He handed the microphone back to James who had expected more information.

Taking the mike back, James recalled the question. "The Oregon Constitution lists qualifications for governor. The age requirement used to be 30, but the voters lowered the age limit to 25 four years ago which means I'm old enough. Also, the Constitution is silent regarding a college education. Your thoughts, Winton?"

Macho ignored the question, launching into a speech on the Ku Klux Klan and the lynching of blacks which darkened US history for a century after the Civil War.

The next question from the audience: Should college education be free?

"Yes," Macho said. James responded, "If college education was free, how should it be paid for?

"The state budget depends on taxes Oregonians pay. If college was free, where would the millions of dollars that would require come from? Winton, what do you say?"

"Taxes should go up. The need should be met," Macho said.

"I disagree. Oregon already has one of the nation's highest state income taxes. Just asking for more is one answer. It's not the one I would choose, and I think most taxpayers would agree with me."

Just off stage Don Lawson had cringed when James veered off the campaign script. Now he was glad James had invited Winton "Macho" Stark to join him. One local television crew was filming the exchanges and Don realized the entire UO campus visit had turned into a win for the campaign.

We've had enough. Let's stop while we're ahead, he thought. He signaled James to thank the crowd for coming. It was time to close the meeting and for them to start for the next campaign stop. A moderate clapping of hands followed as he shook hands with Macho and left the stage.

As the calendar moved through October his backers were pleased to find him gaining in the polls. In the final polling before November 6, and Governor Beckwith-Schall were running neck and neck.

With the largest number of ballots to count, Multnomah County was the last in the state to complete its tally. By Thursday the outcome was clear. James Bonner had won the governorship, his margin of victory exceeding the remaining ballots to be counted in Multnomah County.

That evening a crowd of 500 gathered at the Bonner home in Forest Grove. A television sound truck from Portland provided enough electricity on an evening where the power had failed again.

Lisa and the children flanked James as he thanked the crowd and delivered a short talk. He told him he would work hard to accomplish the goals he had outlined in the campaign talks.

The crowd roared its approval and the TV crew was about to unplug the microphone when his son Skip's voice cut in. "Dad. You're unzipped," he told the audience.

James looked down, saw there was no problem and turned back to Skip who gave him a thumbs up and a big grin.

The crowd laughed. Random voices wished James well in Salem as people started back toward their homes. Their future suddenly looked brighter.

Chapter 12

Life in the Marble Palace

JAMES WAS SWORN INTO OFFICE AS GOVERNOR ON THE SECOND Monday in January. Lisa came to the House chamber on that day and was seated under the vote count scoreboard to watch James take the oath of office and deliver a short address to House and Senate members also being sworn in as state legislators that day. Lori and Skip watched the ceremony later through a cell phone that had recorded the event.

After the oath taking, Lisa joined James, Don Lawson and well-wishers in the ceremonial room entry to the capitol's executive branch offices. After 15 minutes of handshakes and good luck well wishing, James, Lisa and Don broke away from the small crowd. They retreated to the small cramped private governor's office squeezed into a corner of the original 1938 capitol building.

They were about to start on ham and cheese sandwiches Lisa had brought from Forest Grove when they were interrupted by a woman who introduced herself as freshman State Rep. Gloria Martinez from Springfield.

"You helped get me elected," Rep. Martinez said.

"Really?" James replied. "How did I do that?"

"Last May I won the Republican nomination in the primary because in Springfield it was worthless and no one else wanted it. After your visit to Eugene, people started asking me if I supported you and I told them I did because what you said made sense.

"The Lane County Republicans disowned me at that point, but I was still on the ballot after winning the primary.

"After that, outsiders offered to help me with contributions and volunteer work. I raised enough money to pay for a mailer reaching every home in my district. Volunteers canvassed door to door. On election day the four-term incumbent found himself out on the street.

"Governor, the ruling party, the Ds, have a veto-proof majority in the Senate, but the House is different. The Republicans picked up some seats around the state, so the new lineup is 35 Ds, 24 Rs, and one independent, me. That gives your veto power some clout.

"I presume you know—it's no secret in this building—the House and Senate leadership wants to make your life miserable. They want to stymie your agenda, especially where public employee pension reform is concerned.

"I just want you to know I want to help you anyway I can."

"I really appreciate that, Gloria. May I call you Gloria? I want you to meet my executive assistant, Don Lawson, and my wife Lisa. I also want you to know my door is open to you anytime you want to talk to me."

Gloria Martinez declined the offer of a sandwich and took her leave. She had to check out her office in the House wing—the one farther from the floor of the House of Representatives than any other.

The next day James met the legislative leadership—House Speaker Ron Lake and Senate President Tish Papperandeoux.

They told James the budget Don Lawson had produced with the help of professional Statehouse fiscal staff officers was dead on arrival in the legislative branch. It did require public employees to pay $100 million more of their earnings into the pension fund while shifting money to elementary and community college classrooms.

The governor's proposed budget also sliced $8 million from the "feed bill," i.e., the biennial appropriation for the Legislative Assembly. The $8 million cut eliminated salaries of majority and minority party office staffs whose primary function was to help re-elect each party's incumbents in the next election.

Instead, Lake and Papperandeoux explained, they proposed raising the state income tax rates to finance both public employee pensions and more classroom teachers.

"I have a suggestion," James said. "You pass your tax increase and send it to the voters in a special election in May. If they say 'yes,' you win. If they vote 'no,' then your budget committee (the House and Senate Joint Committee on Ways and Means) can put together a real budget.

"The state's next biennial budget begins operating on July 1. I'm sure your budget writers can do the job in six weeks. You agree?"

"You son of a bitch," Lake exploded, face flushed. "We'll gut your budget."

James laughed. "Calm down, Ron. My budget is already wiped out. My predecessor spent almost the entire governor's office budget for the biennium in her last six weeks in office. There's not enough money left to cover my salary through June 30, let alone my staff. My proposed budget cuts my salary and my staff's salaries.

"I feel Oregonians are suffering enough following the earthquake. They don't need higher taxes.

"As you both know, the Oregonian Constitution requires state budgets to be balanced. Don't try to bend the spending limit. I'll veto whatever you come up with."

Faced with the certainty of a veto which the House could not override, the legislative leaders took James's suggestion seriously. They passed their proposed income tax increase through both houses and sent it to the voters. The opposition fought back and launched a barrage of ads. Public employee unions backed the measure with a counter barrage of ads, but on May 15 James's prediction prevailed. The tax measure went down 2-1.

In the meantime James reached an understanding with the

House and Senate co-chairs of the Legislature's budget panel, the Joint Committee of Ways and Means. James made his wants clear. He opposed passing parts of the budget prior to May. He wanted major blocks of the budget—education, health, infrastructure expenditures—held in committee until the May election.

Faced with a veto threat, the budget writers got the message. They did not challenge him.

The biennial budget approved on June 28 retained the Legislature's cherished partisan caucuses funding, but it also phased in higher contributions from public employees whose pensions exceeding $50,000 per year. It also funded more State Police including a special force capable of pursuing any future Malvadoes groups.

All through the session Don Lawson managed the governor's office and arranged James's appointments schedule in a way that allowed him maximum time to deal with issues that he wanted to concentrate on.

The two men started each day finalizing up an hourly calendar as they drove from Forest Grove to Salem. Don also coordinated gubernatorial appointments to Oregon's many regulatory and advisory boards and commissions. New faces and new outlooks started showing up on panels ranging from the State Transportation Commission to farm crop boards.

Part of the established routine also guaranteed James time with Lisa and their children. James, to his surprise, found he was beginning to enjoy being governor as his confidence in handling the job grew month by month. At the same time, he looked forward to the end of his four-year term and a return to the life of a private citizen.

Chapter 13

Family Time / Them or Us

One element in the Bonners' family life that emerged as paramount after the first six months of James's governorship was the importance of the time he and Lisa and the children spent together as family.

On weekday nights James spent in Forest Grove, the dinner meal was not rushed. Conversation was encouraged. Lori and Skip were encouraged to talk at length on any topic they chose. Lisa and James listened carefully, offering questions about their activities or their friends if the conversation lagged. If either Lori or Skip had misbehaved that day, the issue was not raised during dinner. It was dealt with either before or later.

James and Lisa made a practice of taking walks with the kids on weekend days. First they circled the neighborhood. As spring days grew longer, they went downtown to the Dairy Queen for ice cream cones. Later they explored the recently reopened Oregon Zoo and the Portland waterfront.

One weekend when James had to return to Salem the family accompanied him. Obtaining a key to the roof of the capitol, they climbed the metal stairway that circled the rotunda tower and emerged on the paved roof under the Golden Pioneer statue. From there they looked out over Salem, the Coast Range and Cascade summits.

On rainy weekends when the family was housebound, the Bonners played board games like Monopoly, checkers and chess which fascinated both Lori and Skip. Both liked to win and struggled with not winning.

"It's just a game," Lisa would remind them. "Calm down."

Early in their child-rearing phase, Lisa and James discussed how best to discipline Lori and Skip.

"It's them or us," James joked during one of these talks. Lisa did not like his phrase or its adversarial connotation.

They were united, however, on the need for rules of conduct Lori and Skip should follow. Lori was a quick learner and seldom caused them problems. Skip, the perpetual motion machine, was a constant challenge. He seemed to take great delight in pushing Lisa's and James's patience to its maximum limit. He also seemed to detect when parental patience was wearing thin. In a way, he felt like he was winning a game.

One day he miscalculated badly. When James returned from Salem that evening, an exasperated Lisa stopped him just inside the front door.

"You need to talk to our son. He has been driving me crazy all day long. He won't do what I tell him to do. He sassed me. He even stuck his tongue out at me this afternoon when I told him to go to his room."

"I'll talk to him," James said. "Where do you keep the paddle you pound blankets with when you hang them out to dry?"

"You're not going to beat him. Please don't do that," she entreated.

"That's up to him. I want him to know I'm really mad at the way he treated you. That behavior is going to stop now."

Securing the paddle, James called to Skip, who was in the back-yard. As Skip approached the kitchen door, his eyes widened when he saw the paddle and the glowering look on James's face.

"Go to your room," James ordered. "You and I need to talk."

Visibly frightened, Skip meekly climbed the steps to his second-floor bedroom. His eyes followed the paddle which he had not seen in his father's hand before. He sat down on the edge of his bed.

Standing directly in front of Skip, James brought the paddle down on the bed with all the force he could muster. The mattress bounced under the blow and Skip cringed sideways away from the blow.

"Skip, did you stick out your tongue at your Mother today?"

The five-year-old stared at the floor and started to mumble an answer.

"Skip, look me in the eye. Did you stick your tongue out at her today? Did you sass her, talk back to her when she asked you to do something?"

Skip squirmed some more, but did raise his face so that he looked into James's angry eyes.

"Yes," he said softly.

"Skip, your Mother deserves better treatment from you. She loves you with every ounce of her being. She does a hundred things a day to help you and protect you from harm. She does not deserve to have you treat her like dirt and I won't tolerate it."

Allowing a long minute or two to let this sink in, James contin-ued. "So what are you going to do about it?"

"I'm going to do better."

"Skip, look me straight in the eye. You're going to treat your Mother better. Right?"

"Yes." Another pause. "Dad, I don't like you being mad at me."

"I don't like being mad at you Skip, but today you crossed a line. Do we understand each other?"

Skip shook his head "Yes."

"Good. Stand up. Give me a hug."

Skip bolted upright and lunged into James's embrace. The five-year-old had tears in his eyes.

"Skip, let's start by you going downstairs and apologizing to Mother for your behavior earlier today. Tell her you are sorry. Promise her you will do better in the future."

James continued. "And when you see Lori, ask her to come up to your room so we can visit for a second."

Skip turned and fled the room. James could hear his footsteps race down the stairs and then low voices. Lori soon joined him in Skip's bedroom.

James asked her to sit down. "Lori, your brother and I just had a serious talk about the way he treated your Mother today."

"Did you paddle him?"

"No, I did not hit him, but I was very clear about the way I want him to behave around his mother in the future.

"Lori, I know you help Mom from time to time. I really appreciate that. I want you to keeping helping your mother and I want Skip to see that.

"I want Skip to learn how to treat Mom by following your example. I hope you both will help her even more in the future as you grow older. I want Skip to see how you treat her. I want you to set the example I want him to follow.

"Lori, you are the daughter every father wishes he had. I love you very much."

Lori looked up at James, stood and threw her arms around him. He in turn drew her close and hugged her back.

Downstairs in the kitchen, Skip apologized profusely to Lisa for the way he had acted earlier in the day. He promised to do better in the future.

"Skip, thank you," she said. "I want you to know I love you very, very much." She bent down and kissed him on the forehead.

"Dinner is almost ready. Can you set the table with forks, knives and napkins?"

Skip jumped at the chance. He set the table smartly, taking care to line up the knives and forks on the opposite side of the plates as protocol dictated.

Lisa smiled. "Call your Dad and Lori. Tell them it's time to eat."

Chapter 14

Gloria Martinez

Gloria Martinez was not happy as the legislative session got underway. As an independent she had no party caucus to turn to for guidance or support.

Surprisingly, Speaker Tish Papperandeoux did not appoint her to serve on any committees, a development she deeply resented. Also, on the first three occasions when she signaled Papperandeoux that she wanted to speak to the House of Representatives, the speaker ignored her.

When Gloria was refused the third time, she left the chamber fuming and walked down the second-floor corridor and turned into the Governor's office. Told by the receptionist that Governor Bonner was touring the Oregon Correctional Institute, she turned to go when Don Lawson spotted her.

"Come on in," he suggested. They settled in his office and shared an aging pot of coffee. Martinez poured out her anger and frustration. Don listened to her vent and set his cup down.

As he listened, Don studied the new legislator carefully. He noted her Native American, probably Mestizo skin color and jet-black hair, her compact 5-foot-1-inch body, the way she talked with her hands as well as her voice, the strength she projected and depth of her feelings as she spoke.

"Gloria, Papperandeoux may be doing you a favor, one she may come to regret."

"How is that?"

"With no committee meetings you are expected to attend, you can pick a committee that has an interesting agenda. Frankly, I would spend time in Ways and Means as it grinds its way through the state budget. That's an excellent way to learn all the things a state government does and does not do. If I were in your position, that would be my Choice B on any day you do not have a priority bill you are tracking in another committee.

"Also, it's a long-standing courtesy in the Oregon Legislature that if a legislator testifies in a committee meeting, he or she is first in line in giving testimony. Just remember to organize your thoughts in advance, be concise and hold your testimony to five minutes."

"That sounds like excellent advice."

"Gloria, do you have one or two priority bills you would like to see this legislature adopt?"

"There is one I have asked Legislative Counsel to draft. It would change Oregon's partisan primary election into a system like California and Washington have. All candidates for a position would appear on the primary ballot. Every voter would receive the same ballot. If no candidate receives 50% plus one of all the votes cast, the top two candidates who received the most votes would face off in a November general election runoff."

"A superb idea in my view. Your bill will go nowhere in this legislature. It probably won't even get a hearing, but that may be an advantage. It gives you free time to talk up the idea around the state and also draws public attention to you. Finally, Oregon does have the initiative route to the ballot. If your idea draws the interest I think it will, I can see it being put before the voters directly and I also believe you would not have a problem raising money to wage a statewide campaign."

"Don, thank you. You've made my day."

Gloria Martinez made her way to Legislative Counsel to see how close her bill was to being ready to introduce. She spent the afternoon in the Ways and Means subcommittee dealing with education. In the next few days, she smiled a lot when she encountered her fellow House members and gave her first testimony before a Senate Committee discussing a mental health bill.

Two weeks later a House page handed her a note from Governor Bonner asking her to stop by his office. When she did, he asked her about progress on her primary election bill and then handed her a list of four individuals expressing interest in running for office under a new party loosely called the Realists.

"I'm going back to private life at the end of this term," James pointed out. "Unless you plan to do the same, you are positioned to turn Oregon's politics upside down. So go for it."

Go for it, Gloria Martinez did. A year later she had recruited or helped recruit no fewer than 28 candidates to run for the State House and Senate on a non-party basis. She also had cobbled together a statewide network interested in her "Let Everybody Vote in the Primary" cause.

After the election-year short legislative session ended, James Bonner invited her to stop by his office again.

This time both James and Don Lawson were there. They showed her results of a statewide poll which showed her name was recognized by one fourth of those contacted by the poll and two thirds of these respondents viewed her favorably.

"Gloria, have you ever considered running for a higher office?" Don Lawson asked.

"Not really. What makes you think I should?"

"This poll shows you might do well, say, as a candidate for secretary of state. That office supervises elections," James pointed out.

"Gloria, if you decide to run, I believe you can raise money to wage a statewide campaign. I have followed your voting record during the session. You are not locked into anyone's 'camp.' Your votes reflect how I believe most Oregonians think. You also have earned a reputation as a legislator for not rushing to take positions on issues, but when you do commit, you don't waffle. People respect that," Don said.

"Do you both feel I should run?"

Both men nodded yes.

"Gloria, you have been trapped in a no-win position in the House. The election of one or two more independents probably won't improve your ability to move legislation in the next Legislature. As secretary of state, you would have real clout to move Oregon in ways you want it to go.

"And, finally, I don't plan to seek a second term. As secretary of state, you would be in a strong position to run for governor," James concluded.

"Here is a scenario," Don outlined. "You recruit a candidate to run for your House seat in Springfield. You announce you are considering your options for the future and I will suggest to potential donors that they don't commit in the secretary of state's race too early.

"After the primary election you determine the relative strength of the Democratic and Republican nominees. Polling will give you a clear picture of their electability. At that point you will know whether your candidacy makes sense. If you decide to run, I will organize nominating conventions of 1,000 registered voters like we put together for James two years ago and you will be on the November ballot."

"Let me think about it. I'll give you an answer when I decide," Gloria promised.

Six candidates filed for the Democratic nomination to replace term-limited Vincent Rossi of Salem. The winner was Pamela Williams, a Multnomah County Commissioner backed by public employee unions, but whose skills as a campaigner had not been seriously tested in past elections.

Republicans nominated Cave Junction logger Peter Upton, a far-right ideologue who proclaimed a meteor was on its way to strike the earth, potentially ending all humankind.

Gloria Martinez announced her candidacy two weeks after the primary elections. Four separate conventions each drew the required 1,000 registered voters. Money flowed into her campaign after an initial joint appearance by the three candidates before the City Club of Portland. Gloria charmed the audience with answers that were short and concise. She clearly outshone her two opponents focusing on her "Let Every Voter Vote" initiative. It resonated.

Like James two years earlier, Gloria slowly gained ground in pre-November polls. On Election night she led the field but did not claim victory because Multnomah County still had 121,000 votes to count.

Three days later came the final tally: Martinez 40%, Williams 39%, Upton 20%.

At the same time, an initiative to change Oregon's primary nominations system swept the state with a solid 58% yes vote.

James and Lisa attended Gloria's victory party in Springfield. Driving home to Forest Grove through a heavy rain later that night, they both were very happy. A return to a private civilian life beckoned.

Chapter 15

The Dominion of Columbia

Reviewing a growing number of emails in the days after the November election, James was interrupted by a telephone call from his Washington counterpart Quinn Johansen.

"James, you'll be getting a call from Rajit Jain, premier of British Columbia. He wants to get together with you, me and Joyce Simpson, governor of Idaho. He is inviting the three of us, our wives and children to come to Victoria between Christmas and New Year's as his guests.

"He wants us to headquarter at the Fairmont Empress Hotel where we, the governors, can discuss common issues, potential solutions and possibly set up a cooperative arrangement that would benefit all of us. Our wives and children can enjoy Victoria. We would plan on working in the morning and joining them for fun in the afternoons and evenings.

"Rajit also mentioned B.C. Hydro has a lot electricity going to waste at the moment and he wouldn't mind selling some of it across the border if we are interested in buying."

"Well, that's an interesting idea. The Bonners don't have any specific plans for after Christmas and the Legislature doesn't meet until the second week in January," James noted.

"Quinn, how do you plan on traveling to Victoria?"

"By boat, probably the Black Ball Ferry from Port Angeles. It's back up to a once-a-week schedule now."

"I'll talk it over with Lisa. I think our kids are old enough now to enjoy it. I have never been to Victoria. I hear good things about it. I'll let you and Rajit know after we've discussed it here.

On December 28 the premier and Northwest governors and their staffs convened in the Empress Hotel's cavernous 9,100-square-foot Shaunessy Room.

Meanwhile, their spouses and families spent the day exploring the wonders of the world renowned Royal British Columbia Museum across the street from the Empress.

James had Don Lawson accompany him to the meeting.

"Think the room is big enough?" Don asked as he viewed four tables drawn up in a square in the middle of the void. The tables were flanked with rows of chairs. Behind the B.C. flag 27 men and women, representing portfolios in Rajit Jain's government, were taking their seats. A dozen bureaucrats from Washington State were seated on their left. Only two Idaho officials were present. Oregon brought only Don Lawson, who took a seat behind and slightly to James Bonner's left.

Coffee, tea and sweet pastries and fruit were offered conference participants on a linen table-clothed sideboard. Technicians arranged microphones and cameras as the 9 a.m. starting time neared.

Premier Jain opened the session, welcoming his guests and then introducing the small army who sat behind him. He then turned to James Bonner who was seated to his right.

James introduced himself and Don Lawson. He would like to have invited more Oregonians, but this conference was not a line item in his governor's budget. Don, he added, would be in contact with the government in Salem and would obtain information from Oregon that the conference desired. After Governors Johansen and

Simpson completed their introductions, the session got down to business.

First up: the major challenges each of the four executives faced today—six years after the earthquake and the turmoil that swept the military junta into power in Washington, D.C. and Ottawa's growing difficulty in defending its outlying Arctic regions and its increasing disconnect with its west coast.

"Federal payments from Ottawa arrive sporadically or not at all. The province's social safety net is broken, a catastrophe for many citizens," Jain explained.

James started his litany with his so-far limited success in controlling public employee pension costs which continued to drain state revenues away from education and social services that Oregon state government supports. Both he and Quinn Johansen cited ongoing problems with unreliable electricity grids which are costing their states' economies and their residents' incomes dearly. They also outlined problems caused by infrastructure damage caused by the earthquake that have not been repaired.

By 11 a.m. the governors were ready for a break and Jain announced one, adding that a luncheon would be brought in at 11:30. The gathering rose to its feet and several side conversations got underway.

That evening the governors and their families were dinner guests at the home of a friend of Rajit Jain's on Dallas Road overlooking the Strait of Juan de Fuca. Rain and low clouds made Washington's Olympic Peninsula across the strait invisible, but the guests sampled a five-course meal of Indian specialties. Afterward the governors and their wives enjoyed coffee and liqueurs in the home's spacious library while the young children and teens let off steam in a pint-sized gym on the back side of the house. Skip Bonner was thrilled to play badminton with real badminton racquets and shuttlecocks. It was the high point of his day.

The following day, the conference turned to potential solutions to problems identified the day before.

James Bonner and Quinn Johansen expressed a desire to draw upon B.C. Hydro's surplus electricity and the discussion shifted to the need for building new transmission towers and lines to bring the electricity south.

Rajit Jain brought up a new issue: Security. He said B.C. fishermen were encountering aggressive competition from Chinese trawlers in their coastal waters. Two small fishing boats operated by Haidas had nearly been rammed by larger Chinese craft. The Haidas wanted protection of both their fishermen and the fishing stocks they feared the Chinese were depleting. They were threatening to retaliate, a move likely to generate an escalation neither B.C. nor Canada were equipped to handle. The small Canadian naval force based in Esquimalt just west of Victoria had been dispatched north, but by the time they arrived the Chinese had slipped away, their hulls loaded with salmon, cod and halibut.

By the conference's third and final day, the conferees had reached a consensus that some form of new government entity should be created to deal with problems they shared. All four also knew no immediate help would be forthcoming from the United States or Canadian governments. So some sort of new arrangement made sense, even if they had to yield some of their own local powers to make it happen.

Rajit Jain recalled that the four British colonies north of the United States had reached a similar conclusion in 1867. They felt they would be stronger united rather than remain separated. The Americans had invaded twice. They might come a third time having just won a civil war with one of the world's biggest battle-tested armies available for recall.

Initially, the title "Kingdom of Canada" was proposed for the new entity. It was rejected as waving a red flag in the face of Republicans running the United States at that time.

"They came up with the title *Dominion of Canada,*" Jain said. "No one was quite sure what a 'dominion' was, but it worked. The

Americans did not invade a third time. Canada kept the title for almost a century.

"So what about *Dominion of Columbia?*" he proposed. "It would suffice until the US and Canada got their acts together if that took five years or one hundred."

No one came up with a better suggestion, so the governors and premier took the concept and name home and submitted the issue to their respective legislatures for acceptance or rejection.

"Well, what do you think?" Don Lawson asked James as they headed home to Oregon.

"If B.C. power can keep the lights on 24 hours a day, seven days a week and my cell phone works reliably, I'm all for it," James replied.

Chapter 16

So Who Is Gonna Run It?

Other than questions about the new entity's power to tax, the four legislatures voted to join the new Dominion of Columbia and to launch it with $10 million from their own treasuries according to a 4-3-2-1 formula. Washington put up $4 million, B.C. $3 million, Oregon $2 million, Idaho $1 million.

A group of scholars led by law deans in the four jurisdictions wrote a proposed charter including citizens' rights along a two-house legislature, a small executive office and a high court which would handle only legal issues directly linked to the new Dominion government. The "Parliament's" lower house, designated the National Assembly, would have 125 members elected by the people. A 24-member Senate appointed by the legislatures of the three participating states and one province.

All this was accomplished in a few weeks time, but one major question remained unresolved. As Don Lawson phrased it: "So who is gonna run it?" A consensus emerged quickly: James Bonner.

The leaders of Washington, B.C. and Idaho reached out to Don Lawson. How could James Bonner be convinced to take the job given his oft-expressed, consistent desire to return to private life after his four-year term as Oregon's governor ended?

To Don, James was a logical choice to head the new Dominion as its first governor. He had no interest in a long-term political career. He also had a track record of accomplishing what he set out to do. He could make decisions and he had demonstrated a clear capacity to lead. Don clearly felt his friend was the best choice for the job, a clear-headed latter-day George Washington.

Meanwhile Idaho Governor Joyce Simpson took on the challenge of convincing Lisa Bonner that moving the family to a new home in the Seattle area could be good for the family as well as the newly formed Dominion.

Her campaign started with a phone call late one afternoon.

"Hi, Lisa, Joyce Simpson here. How are you and Lori and Skip doing?"

"Well, thank you. How about the Simpsons?"

"We're fine except for Sheila. Yesterday she proved a bicycle colliding with a brick wall combined with gravity and skinned knees are not fun."

"Is she hurt badly?"

"No, she'll be fine. The bicycle also survived which means we won't have to buy another one." There was a pause. "Lisa, this is more than a social call. We have reached agreement in Idaho, Washington and B.C. that your husband is the strongest candidate to take on running this new Dominion government. His best qualification is two-fold. He doesn't want the job. He has proven by his record he is fully capable of handling it.

"That's where you come in. If you support him and let him know it will be a joint undertaking, it would be much easier for him to accept.

"Lisa, we all know you'd prefer being back in Forest Grove in private life. The Seattle area, especially in its knocked-down, post-earthquake misery, won't be easy to handle.

"I can promise you this. We have decided that you and the children and your home will be secure. You will have police protection 24 hours a day, seven days a week. Think of it as an around-the-clock baby-sitting service at your disposal.

"Also, there is full agreement that the Dominion will pay all your household expenses including rent on a nice home in a nice area. This new position will not become a financial burden.

"Lisa, please think about it. If I can help in any way, call me. Like you, I am a wife and mother. My children are as important, more important than any oath of office."

"Joyce, you have dumped a mountain on me. I need time to think. James and I have to talk about it. Has he been contacted yet?"

"Yes, Don Lawson will let him know our decision and our prayerful hope he will accept the responsibility."

"Joyce, I'll get back to you. I appreciate you telling me about this."

"Lisa, it's the least I can do. I want your marriage stronger, your children happier, you happy at the end of the Dominion, regardless of when that comes."

"Thanks."

Lisa put the phone down. Turning around, she was startled to see James standing in the doorway.

"You've heard. They want me to be the executive in the new government. That means a move to Seattle."

"James, you can handle the job. My concern is the children. I'm afraid they will grow up without a dad involved in their lives.

"Driving home from Salem, I had some time to think. Don did the driving and left me to my thoughts.

"First of all, Seattle is a big city. The earthquake hit it hard. Its economy is an ongoing disaster. The biggest employers are struggling with the ongoing problem of unreliable electricity, a fatal handicap if you're building airplanes or computers.

"If we make the move I want my office close to home, maybe in it. I don't want another round of Forest Grove to Salem."

Sighing, Lisa said, "They want an answer. They need one."

"Sweetheart, let's say we'll do it. And tomorrow we will go north and see what we can find in way of housing. Quinn has volunteered us a good realtor who deals with high-priced rentals. He says they don't have a White House duplicate in Seattle, but they do have some great looking homes, some not too far from downtown."

The next day a Washington State Patrol officer met them at the ferry dock in Vancouver, a block west of the earthquake-destroyed interstate bridge. The collapsed steel structure with its lift towers still blocked the Columbia River's main channel.

He drove the Bonners to Centralia where they switched to another state patrol officer. She took them to Olympia, much of the trip involving county roads with a lack of overhead concrete bridges. In Olympia, Quinn Johansen met them with his sailboat at a restaurant overlooking Budd Bay's marina. After lunch they motored north past Tacoma to the Seattle waterfront where they tied up at Pier 82. After dinner at Six Seven in the Edgewater Hotel, he dropped James and Lisa off at their motel, one that fortunately still had central heat.

After a good night's sleep, Ursula Ringgold, Quinn's realtor friend, picked them up and drove them to Lawton Woods just west of Queen Anne Hill and showed them a four-bedroom, four-bath house looking north over Puget Sound.

Ursula explained the owners had left their furniture in place. They had small children and rooms Lisa chose for Lori and Skip were more than spacious. So was the fenced backyard which stood at the top of a low bluff which shielded it from winter high tides. The owners had decided to remain in New England rather than return to Seattle, Ursula noted.

The Dominion government would pay the rent and taxes and Don Lawson had insisted it also pony up plenty of money to cover entertainment if and when the Bonners hosted important visitors.

"Well, it's certainly spacious," Lisa commented when she and James had a moment alone. "I think we could seal off half this place and get by just fine."

"I'm thinking we could turn two or three rooms into an informal home office where I could work unless it was necessary to go down-

town. Don could come here to start our workday. If our communications functioned, we could run the country from two locations."

The two told Ursula they would take the house. Later that day
James and Lisa returned to Oregon to prepare for their move north
and for James to turn over the governorship to just-minted Secretary
of State Gloria Martinez.

Sworn into office days earlier, Gloria would set a new record in
Oregon's history for serving the least time as secretary of state. Don
Lawson had notified her the minute the offer went to James to lead
the new Dominion government.

She was ready, mentally and emotionally.

Chapter 17

Watching Paint Dry

THE NEW GOVERNMENT WAS LAUNCHED WITH AN ELECTION, A minimum of petty bickering and zero offers of boatloads of money.

The election was straight forward. Voters chose a governor, 125 legislators to serve in a National Assembly. Twelve candidates filed for governor. James Bonner won a majority of the votes cast. The Assembly passed bills which then were reviewed by the Senate. If the two houses failed to reach a compromise, the two bodies would cast a joint vote. The goal was to reach a decision. A joint vote was never required to break a deadlock during the Bonner governorship.

Two days after taking office, James sent a written message to the National Assembly and Senate. His number 1 priority was restoring reliable power throughout the Dominion. That was the key to restoring a functioning economy and a normal life for Northwest residents.

Two other challenges needed immediate attention, he noted. The Dominion faced a sharp rise in poverty since the earthquake. Needs of children should come first in tackling the problem, oldsters second. No one should starve.

The other big challenge was defense. With the US Navy gone

from Puget Sound, the Dominion would safeguard the Bangor nuclear sub base from "outside the fence." Addressing the Chinese-Haida dispute over fish, James recommended the Dominion should start by placing camera mounted drones over the North Pacific. An incident leading to a shooting war had to be avoided.

The National Assembly and Senate quickly chose officers and began work on raising and spending money to finance rebuilding the electrical grid. Together, they enacted small increases in state and provincial income and sales taxes and put four-year sunset clauses on the increases.

James sent a follow-up message to the legislators regarding finances. He would veto any effort toward creating long-term debt. The Dominion, he insisted, had to operate on a pay-as-you-spend basis since, he assumed, it was not a permanent government structure. Responsibility for debts should lie with the state and provincial governments.

Some in Parliament grumbled, but they took him at his word and did not contest his veto threat.

This left the province and three states with the task of using multi-year bonds to finance reconstruction of power lines and restoring infrastructure destroyed by the earthquake.

Six weeks into the new administration, Don Lawson told James he had been contacted by a newly opened bank in Seattle. Its officers wanted to meet with James to discuss financing infrastructure.

James agreed to a meeting. He also told Don to check with long-established Northwest banks to learn what they knew about the new bank, the Columbia Friendship Bank. He also cautioned the state and provincial treasurers not to make any commitments with the new bank until more was known about it.

Don soon learned two things. Several long-established banks also showed interest in underwriting the rebuilding costs. In contrast Columbia Friendship Bank was a totally unknown entity. When he and James sat down to work out a plan for interviews and dealing with proposals, they produced a schedule for meetings. But backers of Columbia Friendship had to come first.

A new group seeking Dominion financing now emerged, railroads and associated interests. The two rail companies—Burlington Northern and Union Pacific—wanted money to repair earthquake caused damage as well as upgrades of other facilities.

Along with the railroads' request came a letter from the Northwest Rail Passengers Association asking for a meeting. Its president, Archibald Pham of Tacoma, told James and Don that any money diverted to railroads should be linked to improvements in rail passenger services including reopening service between Portland, Oregon and Boise, Idaho. Goodmanson Randall Steel of Portland definitely was interested in building a fleet of new rail passenger cars if the Dominion made sure it got paid.

James's primary focus remained on restoring electrical service throughout the Dominion. A list of service contracts, eight in all between Vancouver, B.C. and Ashland, Oregon, was prepared and put out to bid.

At this point the banks became cautious. They requested more time to finalize their offerings. There was one exception. Columbia Friendship Bank sought an early meeting with no preconditions. This pleased James, but he still hesitated. He still wanted the new bank to provide more details on its organization, ownership and sources of the capital.

All this took time. Days turned into weeks which in turn stretched out into months. New complications arose as old complications were overcome.

James became increasingly impatient as time rolled on. "This is much worse than I thought it would be," he complained to Don one day in August. "We've lost half a year and haven't let a single contract. It's worse than watching paint dry."

Don sympathized, but reminded James that delays were preferable to bungled results. "This has to be done right the first time around. Otherwise, there will be long-term grief."

James was eager to hear Columbia Friendships' proposals but held back over lingering doubts about the bank's ownership and money sources. Information provided by the bank failed to satisfy him and the review panel of advisors he had pulled together to go over proposed contracts. Don, too, became more suspicious of Columbia Friendship as time went by.

In contrast, the passenger rail contracts moved rapidly. Goodmanson-Randall proposed building two-level cars, the lower providing coach seating, the upper a combination of dining and bar cars. Nothing fancy or luxurious but designed to make the trip pleasant. The trains, like those of the Mexican National Railways in the 1970s, would operate on diesel engines allowing each rail car to travel independently. The coach seats would have trays that dropped down in front of each seat, enabling passengers to use them for various purposes just as they had on airliners for years.

The railroads, having suffered sharp declines in interstate freight volumes since the collapse of the US government, bought in, especially since the deal included $175 million for bridge and track improvements.

Those contracts got an early green light. The first new rail cars appeared on the Seattle-Portland line the following summer when trains began operating at two-hour intervals from 6 a.m. to 10 p.m. daily. Fares were lower than expected. The public responded. Passengers traffic soared to the point a reservation system was required after the first month.

Finally in September the bank interviews began. James found the Dominion had two major options.

Columbia Friendship and a new multiple-bank consortium presented the two most complete plans. James went with the latter when he finally learned Columbia Friendship's web of ownerships led to the doors of the Chinese government. Having the Chinese control electrical transmission was not prudent as several African countries had learned. The consortium won the Dominion contracts. The Washington and Oregon legislatures promptly authorized issuing bonds so the long-delayed construction could begin.

Six months later the first electricity flowed south into northwest Washington. James, Lisa and the children took a special train north to Bellingham to see lights restored to pre-earthquake levels.

"It's beautiful," Lisa proclaimed as their train emerged from the Chuckanut Drive coastal strip and the sudden profusion of lights over-powered the senses.

"This is just the beginning. Let's see where we are a year from now," James replied. He wrapped his arm around Lisa's shoulder. He felt good seeing tangible progress becoming visible.

Chapter 18

Life in Des Moines

AFTER A MONTH IN THE LAWTON WOODS HOUSE, LISA WAS dissatisfied. The house itself was fine. The neighborhood, beautiful homes and all, was not.

In the first few days they lived there she took Lori and Skip and started exploring the neighborhood. She knocked on doors, much to the initial concern of the security detail responsible for the family's safety, searching for children Lori and Skip's ages.

What she learned was that there weren't any potential playmates in their immediate block. A 10-year-old boy was the closest, two blocks south. He was not interested in a younger playmate.

She contacted the nearest elementary school, too distant to walk to. The principal's office was eager to enroll new students, but the environment did not feel right for Lisa. She also learned educators in the building were not enthusiastic about parental help. Education should be left to professionals.

Lisa knew she must approach James carefully, knowing he had plenty to deal with in his new job of setting up a government and running a country. His learning curve was steep. Lisa decided not to mention her concerns, at least at first. After all, his plate was more than full setting up a new startup government. After four weeks though, Lisa felt the subject of the family's living arrangement could not be deferred.

After the children were in bed one evening, she and James settled down side by side on a small couch in front of the family room fireplace. James placed a new log on the grate, closed the screen and sat down next to her where he could wrap his right arm over her shoulder.

"Anything special on your mind?" he asked. "You seem distracted this evening."

"I'm not happy here James. And I'm concerned about Lori and Skip."

"How so? Be more specific."

"It's the neighborhood. No children our kids' ages. And the school they will be attending seems cold. The people there don't want parents around. It just doesn't feel right."

"Do you want to go back to Forest Grove?"

"No. That's the last thing I want. It would mean a permanent separation from you. I need you. The children need you in their lives."

"What do you think we should do?" he asked.

"Well, there must be a hundred neighborhoods in Seattle where children are present. There must be schools that welcome parents who want to volunteer their time as aides. Neighborhoods that are safe for young children to visit neighbors. I would like to find one and move there—security protection officers and all."

"Let's find one. If we have to pay rent, we'll pay rent. The Dominion leased this house for a year. Maybe someone else can use it or the lease can be terminated. Maybe it could be used as a guest house for official entertaining when and if that becomes necessary.

"The important thing. I want you happy. I want Lori and Skip happy. We'll find a home in a neighborhood that's better for us."

"I love you," she said, snuggling closer.

"I love you more than ever," James replied. "Take the kids to school tomorrow. You and the security officer take the truck we brought from Forest Grove and start exploring neighborhoods. We've got three more years in this town. I want those to be good years, happy years for you and the two asleep upstairs."

Lisa began her search the following Monday after taking Lori and Skip to school. She and Peter King, chief of the security detail, used the half tank of gasoline in James's truck to explore Queen Anne Hill and then making their way north along Aurora Avenue through Ballard and neighborhoods farther north.

They saw a number of nice homes that were rentals, but for Lisa nothing seemed totally "right" so their search continued north into the suburbs between Seattle and the Snohomish County line. Then she and Peter turned south along the western shore of Lake Washington. A week later they reached the University District around the University of Washington and Capitol Hill.

James was shocked when his gasoline credit card bill arrived in the mail. With gasoline now retailing at $11.99 per gallon, it was staggering. He paid the bill, but said nothing to Lisa. Her search was too important to curtail.

"Maybe we should look south," Peter suggested one day. So they did, skipping close-in neighborhoods known for gang activity and violence.

Finally, in the shore town of Des Moines, Lisa found the home and neighborhood she sought. A complex of schools was close by. The schools ranged from elementary to high school. A ravine bordered the back side of the house, affording them privacy in the backyard when they wanted it. When Lisa and Peter pulled James's truck up to the curb and parked, they were hailed by two women who were talking across the street. They walked across the street as Lisa and Peter climbed out of the truck.

The women introduced themselves, Ophelia Jones and Marty Ponzi.

"Are you and your husband looking for a house to rent?" Marty asked. "I see your Oregon license plate and thought that might be the case."

"My husband and I are looking for a home to rent. Peter here is not my husband, just a friend," Lisa added.

Peter smiled, but said nothing. I guess Lisa and I are friends in a sense, he thought.

The women told Lisa the house had been occupied for many years by a retired couple who had recently died. They were very nice folks who were happy being surrounded by families with young children. Older kids in the neighborhood did chores for them which helped them stay in the house rather than move into assisted living.

"It's a nice home, three bedrooms and one and a half baths," Ophelia said. "The backyard is enclosed.

"Are there young children here?" Lisa asked. "I have two and I'm looking for a neighborhood where they can play with children their ages.

They women laughed. "Well," Marty said, "There are at least a dozen in this block."

Lisa realized she had not introduced herself. "I'm Lisa Bonner."

Marty suddenly connected the dots, her eyes going back to the Oregon license plate on the truck. "Lisa Bonner. By any chance is your husband James Bonner, governor in the new Dominion?"

"He is, but I hope that won't keep us from being friends," Lisa added. "We want to live here like normal people live. I do have to warn you though. Part of being a governor is having security guards around. One will be here parked at the curb whenever any of us is home.

"Crime and home break-ins are not a problem here," Ophelia said. "As neighbors, we keep a lookout on our neighbors' homes. Anything suspicious, we call the police, and they show up.

"I grew up on the south side of Chicago. I'm one- quarter black so I've seen my share of crime and of bad cops. We have a good local police department. I hope your security officers are not a solution looking for a problem when it comes to people of color," she concluded.

Peter reached into his wallet, drew out a business card and handed it to Ophelia.

"Let me reintroduce myself, Peter King, on loan from the Washington State Patrol and chief of the Dominion's security force. Our primary responsibility is providing safety for Governor Bonner and his family.

"If you ever have a problem with one of my officers, I want a phone call immediately," he said.

Ophelia took the card and thanked Peter. The women took their leave and Peter and Lisa inspected the inside of the house. A week later a moving van brought their furniture to the house.

"Des Moines! I thought that was in Iowa," Don Lawson exclaimed when James informed him about the move.

"This Des Moines is in south King County, Don. It's a nice area. Lisa loves it and Lori and Skip have children their own ages they enjoy being with.

"By the way, the neighbors are welcoming us with a block party this coming Sunday. If you're open, why don't you join us. It starts at 3 p.m. The weather is supposed to be good."

As time passed by in their new home, James agreed with Lisa that moving to Des Moines had been an excellent decision for the family. Skip and Lori were very happy with their new friends. Even the security detail proved popular with the kids. When an 11-year-old hit a ball that broke a light next to a walk-way and the hitter's parents told him he would have to earn money needed to replace the light, the officer who was umpiring the game joined the hitter's team mates in contributing money for the replacement.

When extension of the new power lines south restored around-the-clock electrical service throughout King County, James and Lisa skipped the massive celebration with spectacular fireworks on the Seattle waterfront. Instead, they opted to join their neighbors in a celebratory barbecue in their blocked off street.

Lisa was pleased when Lori developed an interest in art. She loved her elementary school teachers and was an apt student. She vetoed Skip's invitation to participate in flag football but signed on as one of the mothers providing soft drinks at his soccer matches. James and Lisa watched a lot of soccer as their son's skills improved along with his enthusiasm for the sport.

As his four-year term as governor entered its final 12 months, reaching a decision about going home to Forest Grove kept getting deferred. They all were very happy.

Chapter 19

Flags and Drones

ONE LATE SPRING DAY WHEN PERFECT WEATHER SETTLED OVER Puget Sound, James and Don took an extended lunch hour which included a walk along Seattle's waterfront. Their conversation shifted from current problems they faced in running a country to lighter subjects including their teenage years in Forest Grove.

Pausing for a traffic light, James asked, "Don, what do you think are our greatest accomplishments in public life so far?"

"Flags and drones," Don replied. Both men laughed.

"Jim, the flag episode showed me you were a really good politician in spite of what you say. As I recall, choosing a flag for the Dominion was, as you phrased it at the time, 'priority 9924.'"

"You appointed a committee, carefully balanced between the three states and the province, told them to seek designs for the flag and then meet and come up with a final suggestion. You also told them to keep the flag simple and inexpensive. You didn't want to waste money, time or energy on a flag."

James laughed. "I also made it clear I would accept their decision. If some felt it was a lousy flag, they could blame the committee, not me."

"Exactly, you played it just right."

"Then there were the drones," Don continued.

"That was more serious, a real matter of education."

"True. But there were humorous moments—like the teenager from Redmond who offered to build us a super drone that could sink an aircraft carrier if we just named the drone after him."

"I just remember a conference call with the governors and premier explaining that we felt drones could be useful advance warning systems that would allow us to take some defensive measures —like climbing under the bed."

They both laughed again.

"That's when I really appreciated Joyce Simpson. She said she wasn't worried about an attack from Utah or Montana, but noted Idaho could use additional drones for detecting forest fires or locating lost hikers."

"She talked the Boise legislature into a full appropriation on that basis and the other governors went along with the usual 4-3-2-1 formula.

"Intuit was very helpful and gave us a good price on a fleet of small drones and a dozen long-range models that allowed us to probe 400 miles offshore," James recalled.

"And the Haidas ordered two medium-size drones that came equipped with explosive packages that would detonate once attached to the side of a ship," he added.

"They wound up using one of them against a latter-day pirate ship from who knows where—the Malacca Straits?—that tried to board the ferry from Prince Rupert," Don recalled.

"I'm just glad they got the pirate ship, not the ferry," James said.

"Right, but then they asked us if we could provide a replacement so they could patrol the coast down to Bella Bella," Don noted.

The Haidas got a replacement drone that came without the explosive attachment. And the Dominion bought and deployed a fleet of observation craft that eventually numbered 48 drones. A network of drone bases housed in single-family home garages patrolled the entire west coast from Brookings, Oregon north to Nootka Sound. Later in James's second term, the Dominion's drone warning system proved critically important in avoiding an incident that could have triggered World War III.

Chapter 20

I Hope You'll Run Again

AT THE END OF SUMMER IN THE THIRD YEAR OF JAMES Bonner's Dominium governorship, he and Don Lawson were closing down the office before a three-day weekend when Don handed him an envelope and a hand-written letter. The envelope was postmarked Medford, Oregon.

James pulled out the letter and read:

Dear Governor Bonner. When you became governor three years ago, the world my family and I knew was totally screwed up. We were hungry most of the time. There was little or no work. The lights were out. I had no real hope for the future.

Today, everything is better. You made it happen. The future looks great. I know you want to stop being governor, but I hope you change your mind. I know I'm not alone when I hope you will continue leading us. I hope you run again.

s/ Betsy Chang, senior, South Medford High

James carefully folded the letter and placed it back in the envelope. He wanted Lisa to see it.

"You know, James. A lot of people hope you will stick around. The latest polls show your approval rating with likely voters is in the stratosphere. Where your support is weakest—east of the Cascades—it's still 60% positive.

"And, what bothers me is that there is no Plan B, someone on the horizon really capable of taking your place. Look at Parliament, good legislators, but not much executive material as I see it. The governors? All are happy with their present positions. The other day I asked Gloria Martinez what she thought. She said she had no desire to run the Dominion. Just reelected to a second term, she said she was very happy in Salem and wanted to stay there."

She paused. "Of the four governors who backed you three years ago, only Rajit Jain is readily available and he just got voted out of office as you know. Rajit will be stepping down as his party's leader before the B.C. Legislature opens its next session. He said he doesn't see a Canadian leading the Dominion. He called it a 'dumb-ass idea.'

"Incidentally, this is B.C.'s year to host the annual governors' meeting. The new premier, Collin Peterson, wants us to come to his home town, Revelstoke. That's a great area for a family vacation, a lot of outdoor recreation choices," he said, "And he is looking forward to meeting you."

"One step at a time, Don. I told Lisa to plan family time this summer. Does the B.C. invitation conflict with commitments we already have made? If not, tell Mr. Peterson we'd love to come."

There were no conflicts and the Bonners, accompanied by Don Lawson, had a wonderful time.

The conference was headquartered in the historic Pathfinders Hotel, which proved a perfect setting for their small meetings. Their families enjoyed a rooftop hot tub designed to soothe skiers' muscles after a day on the slopes and ate in an outstanding small restaurant. Lisa and James and the children hiked nearby mountain trails. Lori and Skip had their first experience with canoes without mishap, even though Skip got a lesson in balance when the canoe he was leaving went sideways as he climbed back on a dock.

Don meanwhile spent his time cultivating contacts with his counterparts in the new B.C. government. He caught up with Premier Peterson in the bar after dinner on the second night of the conference. Over a high-grade scotch and water, he asked Peterson who he felt should follow James Bonner when his term expired.

"I understand James wants to return to private life, but I hope he changes his mind." Peterson said. "He has been an excellent leader and B.C. has prospered under his guidance. We still have Ottawa tied up dealing with a new Quebec separation campaign, so I feel B.C. should stay with the Dominion for the time being. Before we leave Revelstoke, I will urge Bonner to run for a second term. We will all be better off if he does."

Don thanked Peterson. The pressure on James was building slowly, but surely.

In the months following the Revelstoke conference, James and Don and several of their close friends mounted a serious effort to locate potential successors. What they found was no one with real qualifications wanted a dead-end political career. Also, no new potentially talented, politically committed challengers with proven leadership skills emerged.

James became increasingly frustrated as the months rolled by. He continued to be bombarded with requests that he continue as governor for another four years. Don watched the pressure build and said little.

Suddenly, an unexpected push for James to continue in public life came from a new quarter: his children.

Lori came home from school one day and told Lisa and James she had been invited to lead her elementary school's art club and annual fundraiser.

"Should I turn it down since we will be moving back to Oregon next year?" she asked her parents.

"Do we really have to move?" Skip chimed in. His memories of friends in Forest Grove had faded after four years. He had built a network of new friendships at school and through soccer. He did not want to give them up.

James and Lisa had several long discussions including one on a long weekend by themselves on San Juan Island.

Eventually they concluded James should try for a second term. Possibly they could cut four years short when Skip entered middle school. In the interim they could schedule more time in Forest Grove to allow the children to start rebuilding friendships there.

James notified his former business partner, Alex Martinez that he would not be returning to join him in the construction business for at least two additional years. Alex said he understood, but the partnership would resume as soon as James gave the word.

James then turned to Don and said he would be a candidate for re-election. Elated, Don promised he would not lean on James to consider an additional term in the future. He had James compose a statement which he released to the media:

"Today I have decided to seek a second term as governor of the Dominion. Together with your support, we have accomplished much in the last four years. With your continued support we can achieve even a better future for ourselves, our families and our neighbors in the next."

The campaign turned out be a cakewalk. Six other candidates, including a Washington State University freshman, filed. James swept the field taking 74% of the total vote.

On election night the Bonners celebrated the victory at a neighborhood potluck following another one of Skip's soccer games. As James and Lisa climbed into bed, they hugged and kissed.

"You know," he said, "a lot of second terms don't turn out well. In our case I hope history doesn't repeat itself."

Chapter 21

Teen Challenges

LORI BEGAN HER TEENAGE YEARS WITH ANTICIPATION, HOPE AND growing concerns about her health, especially dealing with the transition from girl to woman.

She kept her thoughts and feelings to herself for several months, but eventually broached the subject to her mother. Lisa immediately took Lori to the back porch of the house away from Skip and his two friends who were shouting to each other over a board game.

"Lori, you are experiencing changes your body that are totally normal as a female child starts becoming a young woman.

"Every girl goes through this. For some the transformation starts at an early age. For others it begins later."

Lisa went on to explain step by step what Lori should expect to see and feel as months went by. She told Lori her flat chest would change as her breasts developed and grew, sometimes expanding dramatically. Based on her experience and her recollection of her mother and grandmother, she likely would not have overly large breasts. Menstrual cycles would begin. Either way, what she was experiencing was totally normal, Lisa said. She then asked Lori if she had any questions.

Lori had a dozen. Lisa answered each one slowly and carefully, frequently repeating items and facts she had mentioned previously in their conversation.

"What about Skip? Do boys go through this too?"

"Boys go through changes, but in different ways. Skip is younger than you are so he is behind you in the changeover process.

"One thing likely won't change, at least right away," she added. "I have noticed your brother can be really obnoxious. That's not likely to change until he's older."

They both smiled.

"Lori, when that happens let me know. Just tell Skip to get lost when he hassles you. Okay?"

"Also, Lori, let's have another talk like this any time you have a question."

The two stood up and hugged each other. "Mom, I love you so much."

Three weeks later Skip injected himself into Lori's life in a new way. She was approached after school by Jim Dutton, one of her classmates, a tall, athletic boy. Jim asked her if he could walk her home. Lori said she'd like that, but she would have to clear it with the security detail officer assigned to protecting the governor's family. She explained the matter to Dutton who readily agreed once he understood that it was required. The officer would trail 50 yards behind while his co-worker drove Skip home.

All went well until they reached the front door of the house. The door flew open. Skip stood there grinning, a half-eaten slice of bread and peanut butter in his left hand.

"This your new boyfriend?" Skip asked.

Lori started to detonate, but Jim smiled at her. "Hey, kid, do you have a football?"

"Yeah."

"Great. Finish your snack and bring it here."

Skip rushed away and returned a minute later with the ball.

"Can you catch this?" he asked.

"Of course," Skip responded with confidence.

"Show me. Go out for a pass."

Skip ran across the lawn, looked back and up to see the ball sail way over his head. He ran after it and retrieved it 40 yards down the street. Grabbing the ball, he ran back to Jim and Lisa.

"Okay, now run to the yard next door and turn left." This time Skip almost caught the ball, but it slipped through his fingers.

"This won't go on forever," Jim assured Lori. And it didn't. Sweating, Skip returned the ball again seven more times.

"Lori, does this kid have a name?"

"Skip."

"Skip. Do the world a favor. Go inside and leave us alone. Your sister and I would like to talk. Do we understand each other?"

"Yes," Skip replied. He disappeared into the house and closed the door.

This episode repeated itself when Jim walked Lori home again. They stopped when Jim's father was promoted and he and his family moved to Spokane. Then a new boyfriend entered the picture.

His name was Arturo Campino. He was not an athlete. He was tall, thin and wore glasses. He and Lori met through the art club at school. Skip was not impressed. He nicknamed him "Artsy-Farty." He pestered the two of them whenever Arturo was around.

"Mom, make Skip stop being a jerk. Make him leave us alone."

Lisa ordered Skip to go to his room or go outside. Skip complied, but he was back at it the next time Arturo came to the house. Skip was persistent. So was Lisa.

Finally, Lori struck back at dinner one night, the arena where child-parent conversation was encouraged and discipline not mentioned.

"Dad," Lori asked as her father popped a meatball into his mouth, "will Skip be as obnoxious after his balls drop?"

After choking momentarily, James looked at his daughter and replied, "Short term, no. Long term, yes."

"What does she mean?" Skip asked, understanding Lori's question was not friendly, but also not comprehending it.

"That's enough on this subject," Lisa commanded.

A long silence followed. Then James switched the conversation, updating the family on Don Lawson's latest undertaking, learning to sail a 21-footer capable of sleeping four.

After dinner, Lisa and Lori withdrew to have a mother-daughter discussion about suitable dinner-time topics. James invited Skip outside to take a walk. He learned about Artsy-Farty. After a brief discussion about put-down names and the harm they can cause, James responded to Skip's question at the dinner table.

"Balls dropping is a slang phrase referring to a boy becoming a man," he explained. "Part of this process is that a boy's voice changes, becoming deeper.

"In the next year or two you will go through this process. Your testicle sack will hang lower in your crotch and your voice will change. You will notice it when you take a shower or put on your underwear. It's nothing to worry about.

"Skip, Lori is going through a similar process in becoming a woman. Do her, your Mom and me a favor and don't tease her about it.

"Teasing in itself is not bad, but there are limits. Son, you will find that if you treat others, including your sister, with respect, they will treat you with respect. It just makes sense and makes life better for everyone.

"And," he added, "no more Artsy-Farty. I don't want to hear that one again.

Chapter 22

Red Wine and Sex

Don Lawson had two main themes in his life. One was a love of politics. The other for the past five years was assisting his longtime, non-politician friend James Bonner in becoming successful as governor of the Dominion of Columbia.

That focus started shifting in the fifth year of Bonner's governorship. James planned to return to private life at the conclusion of his second term. Don's ties to the government of Columbia and his overall career would change dramatically when that happened.

Don had just emerged from taking a shower late on a Saturday afternoon after working all night the night before and sleeping most of the day when the doorbell rang.

It was totally unexpected since the only time he usually heard it marked the arrival of a pizza.

"Hello," he called into a speaker phone linked to the apartment building's front door.

"Hi, Don. It's Agatha Derwinsky. I'm here with a bottle of Merlot. It's starting to rain and I'm getting wet so let me in, please."

"Agatha, I'm not ready for company."

"Don, this is a social call, not business. I want to see you. So, unlock this door. I'll wait outside your apartment door until you're ready to see me. At least I'll be out of the rain."

Don sighed. What in hell does she want? he asked himself.

He pressed the button which unlocked the apartment building's front door. He heard it buzz so Agatha was inside the building. He hurriedly put on a sweatshirt and a pair of shorts, ran a comb through his hair and unlocked his apartment door.

Agatha breezed in, a smile on her face. She was wearing a tight-fitting sweater and a pair of the shortest shorts he had ever seen. Crossing the room, she placed the bottle of Ste. Michelle Merlot on the kitchen counter, reached into her handbag for a wine opener and opened the bottle "so it could breathe."

Looking around Agatha noted a dearth of furniture—a table and chair and a workbench with Don's closed computer on it. Looking around a corner she saw a single bed in a bedroom.

"You seem a little spartan," Agatha said. "Do you do anything but work and sleep here?"

"That's pretty much it. I don't entertain."

"Show me your bedroom, Don."

"It's around the corner."

"Come here, Don."

As he followed her into the bedroom, she turned suddenly, pushed herself into him and planted a kiss on his mouth. Stunned, Don pulled back, but she grabbed him in the crotch, spun him around and shoved him down on the bed.

"Are you gay, Don?"

"No."

"Then let's have some fun." Pulling down his shorts, she pushed him back on the bed and then fell on top of him.

"Agatha."

"Shut up, Don. Let's see if you are the man I think you are."

Don did not need more encouragement, his body responding to Agatha with surging energy. Rolling over on top of her he entered her. Soon they both climaxed.

For a minute or two they lay next to each other. Then Agatha spoke.

"Don, you were great. After we sample the wine let's do it again."

And they did. The day faded into darkness before Agatha took her leave.

"Next time, my place," she offered. "Are you in town next weekend?"

He made sure he was, making love in her fourth-floor condo overlooking Lake Washington. This time the sex was enhanced by an excellent beef stroganoff and two more bottles of Ste. Michelle. It turned out one of her cousins owned land the winery's grapes grew on.

On good weather weekends, Agatha introduced Don to sailing. Subsequently they spent many weekends on her 21-foot boat, eventually making it to the San Juan Islands when Parliament was not in session and Don's administrative duties did not interfere.

James and Lisa Bonner realized there was a change in Don's life when he stopped sharing his weekends with them. When James pointed out his absence, Don told him about Agatha. They rarely discussed Dominion business, Don assured James. That satisfied James. The two friends worked more closely together than ever.

Chapter 23

Skip's Ordeal

THE MORNING SUN FILLED SKIP'S BEDROOM AS HE RUBBED HIS eyes and focused on the day ahead. It was summer but school would continue until mid-July, still four weeks away.

I really don't want to go to school today, he thought, gazing out the window which overlooked the Bonner's backyard.

He swung his feet over the edge of the bed and started dressing—underwear, a short-sleeved sport shirt and khaki shorts. He was lacing his shoes when his mother summoned him to breakfast. Breakfast was a hurried meal in the Bonner household. His father, the governor, had left for work at sunrise. His mother would drive his older sister to her new school in a half-hour. The Security Detail officer—today Hector Guzman was on duty—would escort Skip to his middle school across the deep ravine that separated the neighborhood and the middle school, driving his patrol car a half-block behind Skip who was walking the route.

Skip hated the whole escort scene. Other kids teased him about it. Like any self-respecting 12-year-old, he did not relish being chaperoned like some small child.

As he finished his cereal a thought flashed through his mind.

What if, instead of walking out the front door of the house as he normally did, he went out a back door, crossed the lawn, topped the fence and cut across the ravine? By the time Guzman checked on him, he would be out of site and on his way.

For sure there would be consequences, Skip knew. His Dad and Mom would not be happy—big understatement. He probably would be grounded for a couple of days, but he also would be sending a message. He was growing up and his parents should recognize that fact.

He devised a plan. Go to school unescorted.

At the outset, it worked beautifully. With at least a five-minute head start, he reached the back fence, climbed over it, dropped to the ground, and started looking for a trail that might lead him to school.

In the ravine Skip could not find a trail and decided to cut down through the brush which grew thicker as he went down the slope. The slope got steeper, and he struggled at times to maintain his balance. Skip got concerned about the time this was taking and he knew Patrolman Guzman would be looking for him by now. Pausing for a second to decide how to work his way through the brush, he heard a twig snap.

Then it happened. Three teenagers jumped him, knocking him face down into the dirt and rocks. They were big and they pinned him on the ground simultaneously groping him in an effort to reach his wallet. Skip struggled, which drew him a kick in the side.

"Damn," a boy with spiky hair muttered. "There's only $10 here —$5 US and $5 Canadian. The way this kid is dressed, there should have been more." That money was not to be spent, Skip's father had told him. It was for emergencies only.

Fueled by a burst of adrenalin, Skip pushed himself upward as the trio contemplated their small haul. He threw the skinny boy off balance temporarily and used all of his strength to break free for a moment. As he stumbled to his feet he was tackled again, but this time one of his legs found a target, the groin of one of the two heavier boys who had dark curly hair and a beard. The 18-year-old howled in pain as he fell backward down the slope until he landed in thick brush.

The other two teens now turned on Skip with vengeance, raining blows with fists and feet all over his body. Slowly the 12-year-old realized he was passing out. His arms fell at his side as he lay on the ground. His body bled from multiple scratches. Still, the blows kept coming as the two boys kept kicking his body.

Then quiet. The straggly blond helped the third boy who Skip had kicked back on his feet and the trio disappeared with Skip's $10.

Meanwhile Guzman, assisted by four other police officers, drove adjacent streets looking for the missing 12-year-old. The Des Moines police dispatcher contacted the school. No, they were told, Skip was not present.

The search zone expanded to a broader circle including the ravine behind the Bonner home. Two teams of searchers started probing the ravine aided by police dogs. News of Skip's disappearance reached Governor Bonner's office in Seattle where James was meeting with a group of cable manufacturers about extending cable service into remote sections of Columbia still dependent on lanterns and gas lamps.

"Keep us posted" was the first response of the head of state. James phoned Lisa to let her know Skip was missing.

Anxiety grew as hours passed and the possibility of kidnapping entered the mental picture. More officers and neighborhood watches joined in. At 12 noon television newscasts posted Skip's picture along with an appeal for help.

At the same time, a door opened in a home five blocks down the street from the Bonners' that also backed up on the ravine. Savali Fautanu, a strapping 225-pound, 19-year-old Samoan, arrived home having bicycled from his service station job for lunch his mother, a housekeeper for the family occupying the home, had waiting for him.

"When you've finished eating," she said, "I want you to do something for me. The TV just announced Governor Bonner's 12-year-old son is missing. After you left the house this morning I heard some sounds that made me feel someone was fighting in the ravine. Can you check it out?"

Not enthusiastically, Savali did what his mother asked. In the ravine he found someone had broken a trail through the brush and followed it down the slope. Well down into the ravine, he found Skip's body. Savali knelt down and took Skip's wrist, checking to see if there was a pulse. There was, barely.

He then carefully turned Skip over. He could see the kid had been beaten severely. His body was covered with black and blue spots surrounded by dried blood from brush scratches.

The next thing Savali knew, two police officers and a huge German shepherd towered above him.

"Don't move," one of the cops said. "You're under arrest."

"I didn't do this," he protested. "I had nothing to do with this. The only thing I did was turn him over so I could try to help him some way."

The officer, having received some blows himself in breaking up brawling Samoans in the past, took no chances. He handcuffed Savali while the second officer summoned paramedic help. Savali, having been arrested for fighting two years earlier, did not resist. He knew the drill.

Within minutes paramedics arrived, checked Skip's vital signs and whisked him away to nearby St. Charles Hospital on Federal Way. Doctors in the emergency room there immediately determined his injuries required more sophisticated care. He was transferred to the recently consolidated University Hospital on First Hill in Seattle.

Meanwhile the police officers who had arrested Savali led him to their parked cruiser and drove him to police headquarters in Seattle. They placed him in a holding cell pending interrogation by detectives. Savali kept hoping to be released once more facts were known. That didn't happen.

When James learned Skip was en route to University Hospital, he phoned Lisa who joined him there. Together the awaited information in the emergency room lobby along with a member of the security detail. As minutes turned into hours they held hands and prayed.

Finally, Dr. Yang Hu appeared and invited them to a small side office. He gave them his report in straight, direct language. Skip had been beaten severely. He had two broken ribs and bruises all over his body including his face and head. Fortunately, an MRI showed no permanent damage to the brain or his eyes, but he was in a coma and would be allowed to stay there for the time being.

Recovery would be a slow, tedious process, Hu advised. More tests would be required, he said. Skip would be monitored around the clock in the Emergency Department and kept in isolation. Absolutely no visitors, Hu said. And Skip should receive no news or have contact with the outside. Skip needed total undisturbed rest. They would be notified when Skip regained consciousness, he told the anxious mother and father.

"Would it be helpful if an armed guard stood outside his room?" James asked.

"Because he is the governor's son that would be appreciated," Hu replied, "with the understanding that the guard would not enter the room under any circumstances. Medical personnel only."

James then turned to the next business at hand, meeting the media who would be hungry for details. He asked Lisa to stay behind in the small office while he went outside a side portico door and confronted around a dozen press—radio, TV reporters, bloggers— assembled behind microphones.

Positioning himself in front of the mikes, James said. "I have a brief statement and I won't take questions at this time. Our son is severely injured. Recovery will take an unknown length of time. The doctors have ordered complete isolation. That means no interviews so don't even try. An armed guard will be outside Skip's room 24/7. Any attempt to disrupt his recovery with an interview or pictures will result in arrest and prosecution backed by the full power of government.

"So, don't try it. Don't ask hospital personnel for help in any way. They fully understand the seriousness of our son's injuries and know if they are linked with any security breach, they will be fired on the spot and their ability to pursue a medical career will come to an end.

"I hope I'm clear. Thank you for your understanding."

Skip's progress toward recovery was glacial, just as Dr. Hu had forecast. Days turned into weeks, but slowly, aided by a string of tests and small surgeries, their confidence grew that Skip would eventually recover fully.

Once Skip regained consciousness, however, he became increasingly agitated about the enforced isolation and more and more vocal about his displeasure. Finally the doctors eased the restrictions and allowed him access to a phone and TV as he gained strength through relentless physical therapy to start rebuilding his mobility, especially his ability to walk.

After several more weeks, the hospital transferred Skip to a private room and that's when he saw a disturbing image on a television newscast. A trial was about to begin for a black man indicted by a grand jury for assaulting Skip. Skip immediately dialed his father's personal cell phone number.

"Dad, they arrested the wrong man," he told James. "I was attacked by three white guys around 17 or 18 years old. There was no black guy present."

James, surprised, said he would contact the King County prosecutors. "They probably will want to talk to you," he added.

But the prosecutors seemed not interested. They thought they had a strong case and the trial, much delayed, was scheduled.

Skip was stunned when James relayed the prosecutors' lack of interest in talking to him.

"Dad, I know nothing about trials and courts, but something is horribly wrong here." After a pause, Skip continued, "What do you know about the black guy? What's his name? Why was he arrested?"

James told Skip the black man was a Samoan who was found next to him when law officers arrived on the scene. The man had a prior arrest record, he recalled. He could not recall the man's name other than the TV newscasters found it hard to pronounce.

"What can we do?" Skip grumbled. "He was not there when I was attacked. Isn't there something we can do?"

"Let me make another phone call, this one to the King County prosecutor. After I reach him, I'll get back to you."

Putting his cell phone down, James paused to think. He knew Thomas Izard was a hard-shell "take no prisoners" attorney who did not welcome unsolicited advice, especially from non-lawyers or politicians. He and Izard had clashed over items in the Dominion's budget on two occasions. James, keeping his cool, had won both skirmishes.

After thinking for a few minutes about how he should approach Izard on his son's request, James phoned him.

"What the hell do you want?" Izard launched the conversation.

"I'm trying to do you a favor," James replied.

"What the hell do you mean. If this is in regard to your son's assault, I have a strong case. The jury will buy it. I'll get a conviction. I always do."

"Izard, either you or your prosecutors handling this case should talk to my son. The doctors will allow you to do that now. He will tell you no black man was present when he was beaten. He will tell you there were three white guys, 17, 18 or so years old who assaulted and robbed him when he was on his way to school.

"I called you because your deputies didn't seem interested and I don't believe blindsiding the number one prosecutor in the state of Washington helps make anyone safer.

"If you don't want to talk to Skip, I bet the Samoan's defense attorney would be delighted to hear what the kid would say in court. So what's it going to be, Izard? What should I tell Skip?"

A long pause followed as reality set in. He knew James Bonner was right.

"I'll send a deputy prosecutor to the hospital," he said.

James ended the call. He phoned Skip to give him the news and then called Lisa to bring her up to speed. He told her he would go to the hospital. He wanted to be present when the prosecutor interviewed Skip. He did not want Skip caught in some legal crossfire.

Two hours later the new prosecutor thanked Skip for talking to him. He told him the charge against Savali Fautanu would be dropped. The matter took a few minutes of the court's time. The judge told Savali he was free to go. There would be no trial.

A month later Skip caught up with James after dinner. "Dad, whatever happened to the Samoan guy who found me after the prosecutors dropped charges against him?"

James paused. "I don't know. What would you like me to do?"

"I'd like to meet him. Could we invite him over or something?

James was cautious. He remembered Savali Fautanu had a police record.

"I'll look into it," he promised.

In the following days Skip was persistent. James eventually relented and sent a letter to the Fautanu home inviting Savali and his mother, Tueila, over for supper on a Sunday evening.

It turned out to be a very pleasant gathering featuring hamburgers cooked on a grill on the back porch. Tueila brought a Samoan salad James and Lisa both enjoyed. They learned Savali's father, a 300-pound lineman, had been drafted by a major NFL team straight out of high school in Honolulu. His professional football career had been cut short by injuries and he had died at age 40, leaving Tueila responsible for raising their son. Savali in turn had made some bad choices in choosing friends and that led to a police record for fighting and reduced career opportunities.

Tueila told James and Lisa Savali was a good son who brought his paycheck home to help cover household expenses, including groceries. He had stayed out of trouble for three years and she was very proud of him.

Skip and Savali had left the discussion early to shoot baskets and then sat down for some serious conversation of their own. Skip mostly listened and asked questions. Savali learned it was fun to play the mentor role for the first time. He enjoyed it.

After the two families got together again a month later, Skip approached James with an idea. Could Savali join the security detail protecting the Bonners? Again, James was cautious, but by this time his appreciation for Savali had also grown. He called the commissioner whose portfolio included the security detail.

"Norm, I'm not telling you how to run your department or who you should hire. On behalf of my son I would appreciate it if the person responsible for hiring officers would at least talk to Savali Fautanu, the man who found my son after he was beaten and tell him what the job requires and the responsibilities that go with it.

"This is the last time I'm going to mention it to you," he concluded.

The department contacted Savali and interviewed him, then hired him on a trial basis. After a six-months' training program, Savali joined the security detail assigned to the governor's family for eight hours a day, five days a week.

Skip never gave the detail any cause to worry about his personal safety until he took up rock climbing on stone cliffs in the Cascade foothills. Rock climbing turned out better than crossing the canyon at age 12.

Chapter 24

A Real Crisis: The Chinese Navy

D RONES OPERATING OUT OF N EAH B AY FIRST SPOTTED A FLEET of navy vessels headed east toward the Strait of Juan de Luca when it was 250 miles west of Cape Flattery.

Report of the sighting reached Port Angeles immediately and was relayed to the capitol. A half-hour later Governor Bonner took a call from Don Lawson. James had just finished a speech to a Yakima service club in which he praised local apple growers for donating much needed food to Puget Sounders after the earthquake. Don told him about a large naval flotilla approaching the coast and told him to return at once. Don met James when his westbound train reached Tacoma. The two of them headed north to rendezvous with national security officials in Seattle.

By then the fleet was nearing the coast. It was the Chinese navy. Early the next morning, the drones reported a jet fighter had been launched from the *Laioning,* the oldest carrier in the Chinese fleet. An English-speaking pilot requested permission to land in Victoria which had a runway long enough to accommodate his jet.

British Columbia dispatched a military officer, Captain Ian McBride from the navy base in Esquimalt along with a corporal, Paul

Chang, who spoke Chinese, to the airport. Bonner and his advisors waited anxiously for the next message.

Thirty minutes later relief set in. The visit was a courtesy "friendship" visit. The Chinese requested permission to enter Puget Sound and to anchor opposite Seattle. They also asked also if Governor Bonner would meet with Admiral Chiang Yu, who commanded the naval group.

Word was sent back. "Yes" to both requests along with an offer to provide a pilot through Puget Sound. Not necessary, the Chinese replied. The fleet was directed to anchor north of the high-traffic ferry crossings between Seattle and Bainbridge Island and Bremerton and to keep its fighter jets out of the approach corridors north of Seattle-Tacoma Airport. (This request was hardly necessary since Sea-Tac traffic was down to only four flights a day, all coming from Vancouver, B.C.).

Once the *Laioning* and its dozen smaller support craft were anchored, negotiations began over where the meeting between the governor of Columbia and Admiral Yu should take place. The admiral was reluctant to go ashore. James was equally reluctant to go aboard the aircraft carrier. Eventually the two met upon a barge towed to a spot near the carrier. The barge featured lawn furniture seating 12 individuals, outdoor artificial lawn borrowed from a golf course and a tent with raised flaps. Fortunately the sky was clear and the wind calm when the two officials met and shook hands on at 2 p.m. on a Tuesday afternoon. Dragon Green tea and cookies provided by a Seattle grocer provided refreshment for the two leaders and their entourages.

James welcomed Yu on behalf of the government and the people of Columbia and initiated the conversation by asking Yu about his life and career in the navy.

"Do you come from a navy family?" he asked.

"No," Yu replied. He said he was born and grew up in Manchuria after the Korean War, entered the navy as a young man and had risen through the ranks, reaching flag rank while directing construction of bases on islets in the South China Sea while based on Hainan Island.

Yu then asked Bonner about his past, commenting on his rise to power after 'the revolution and overthrow' of the US government in Columbia.

Digesting this question, James concluded (1) Yu was likely more of a political careerist than a navy careerist and (2) he had a distorted take on recent Columbia history starting with the earthquake and its aftermath. There was no revolution in the usual sense of the word, he explained. It was more of a case of abandonment including departure of the military forces that formerly occupied bases in the Puget Sound region. Columbia was created to fill a vacuum when the US government imploded, at least in the Pacific Northwest.

"So what caused you to bring the *Liaoning* to Puget Sound? Is there a purpose for your visit here or does your trip also include stopovers in California or possibly Latin America?"

Each man's eyes locked on the other's. James was smiling when he posed his questions, but Yu sensed he was serious and meant business even though a total amateur in foreign affairs. He'd also felt James Bonner was absolutely serious about protecting his country.

Yu also knew Columbia had no army, navy or air force and its military presence was limited to drones that had tracked his fleet's progress from several hundred miles off the coast.

"China wants peace with all countries," he said. "China is a world power, now indisputably number one economically and militarily. China is interested in trade and is willing and able to provide billions of dollars needed to restore infrastructure destroyed by the earthquake. It also is willing to help Columbia protect itself by installing security cameras that would immediately notify its government of any threat anywhere within its boundaries."

James pondered the latter offer for a moment, thanked Yu for offering it. Columbia did not need security cameras, especially ones that spied on its citizens. He knew Yu did not need a lecture on western democracy or its principles, but he wanted to emphasize a point he was fairly certain the admiral could understand.

"Eight years ago I was a building contractor in a small Oregon town," he said. "Then came the 9.5 earthquake that struck the northwest coast. You can look at the Seattle skyline across the water and see the damage from where we are sitting.

"Compounding the disaster was the collapse of the US government, including Social Security payments which underpinned the American economy. Here in Washington and Oregon anarchy rose along with hunger aggravated by collapsed transport networks.

"I had a role, a small one, in restoring order in my part of Oregon. My neighbors turned to me to help bring back order to their shattered lives which tie communities together. One step led to another, which caused me to be elected governor of Columbia for a four-year term. Last year, after some progress in bringing back electricity and related services, the voters chose me to continue as governor for another four years.

"That's it. Eight years is enough, and I will step down, probably return to my home town and resume building, work I truly enjoy. The people of Columbia will elect a new governor, or, if the federal government goes back to civilian control and resumes services it provided in the past, the American flag will replace the Columbia flag and we will move forward as part of a renewed United States of America.

"China and Columbia have different histories. Each has developed under very different political systems. Our people and your people are alike in many ways, but our governmental structures are very different. I doubt the people of China would like our system. I know the people of Columbia would not like living under the Chinese system which includes surveillance of every citizen," he concluded.

After some additional small talk, Yu asked James about the status of US Navy facilities in Puget Sound as well as the nuclear base at Bangor. Also, he added, China would like a base on the east side of the Pacific to help it carry out its growing worldwide responsibility of preserving peace. China would be interested in building a new base on the south shore of the Strait of Juan de Fuca, perhaps on land granted under a 99-year lease.

So, James thought, this is the real purpose of Yu's visit to Puget Sound. He phrased his response carefully. He explained to Yu that all of the US Navy's facilities on the Sound and Bangor were locked up and had been since the Navy's departure. He explained Columbia monitored those facilities, but any disposition of them would require China negotiating directly with the US government. As for construction of a Chinese base on the Strait of Juan de Fuca, he would present a formal request to his government should one be prepared. He felt it would not be received favorably.

Yu did not respond to these comments directly but soon brought the meeting to an end, saying he had to return to the *Liaoning*.

The next morning the admiral sent a message to James thanking him for their meeting. He reported the Chinese fleet would be leaving Puget Sound and returning to the open Pacific. Two hours later James received another message, this one from Columbia's southernmost drone base at Brookings, Oregon. A Dominion drone had spotted a US Navy battle group heading north. It was 200 miles west of Cape Blanco.

James immediately summoned Columbia's defense leaders to his office and updated them about the Chinese departure and the US Navy's anticipated arrival. After a brief discussion the group decided to keep monitoring the situation its sea by drones keeping well away from the US fleet. The barge that hosted Yu was moved to Tacoma and replaced with one capable of blasting fireworks into the sky in honor of the US Navy's return.

After the meeting broke up, James and Don retreated to James's office. Seated, James leaned back and placed his feet on his desk.

"Damn," he said, "we sure lucked out on that one. I could use a drink, a real stiff one."

"So could I," Don replied. He left the room and returned two minutes later with a fifth of Johnnie Walker Red Label scotch along with a tray of ice. Pouring each of them a glass. he sank into a couch. They each took a sip. James, who rarely drank, coughed.

Catching his breath, he said, "Can you imagine what would have happened if the US force caught the *Laioning* in Puget Sound or Juan de Fuca?"

"It would have another 9.5 earthquake or worse. And a lot of civilian blood shed in collateral damage," Don replied. "I'd rather not even think about it."

"We would have been set back for years. Thank God it didn't happen."

"The question is, will the Chinese come back? And if they do, will the US Navy be here when they do show up?"

Suddenly Don realized James had fallen asleep. He reached over and took the glass with its residue of scotch from James's hand, lowered his feet off the desk and rolled James over to the couch. Reaching under James's shoulders, he lifted his friend up and lowered him onto the couch. He removed James's shoes and put his feet on the couch.

Then he reached for his phone to call Lisa.

Chapter 25

Foreboding

WHEN LISA ANSWERED THE PHONE DON KNEW BOTH HE AND James were in trouble.

"What do you mean he can't come home?" her angry voice demanded.

"I haven't heard from him in four days, ever since this China thing came up. He hasn't seen me or the children. He hasn't even called."

"Don, when I agreed to the second term, I had an understanding. The children and I would be part of James's life and we would be part of his."

Listening and realizing that everything Lisa said was true, Don did not interrupt her even as her voice rose along with her agitation. It was better to let Lisa vent as circumstances gave her every right to do.

Finally, Lisa stopped to take a deep breath before continuing.

"Is this the new normal? Is this what we can expect for the next two years?"

Seeing an opening, Don answered as soothingly as he dared, hoping his voice expressed honesty and sincerity.

"Lisa, you're upset. You have every right to be mad, every justification. Ever since the Chinese were spotted heading for Puget Sound, nothing has been normal. Now that they are gone, James has had enormous pressure lifted off his shoulders. The US Navy arrives tomorrow. They will want to talk to James. After that I'll send him home and cancel any appointments through next week. You need time together."

"Fine, Don. I hope it happens." And with that she turned off her phone. Tears came to her eyes. She sobbed, reached for a tissue, wiped her eyes and noticed for the first time she was not alone. Lori and Skip were standing in the doorway silently, worried looks on their faces. Seeing their mother cry was something they had rarely if ever seen before.

"It's okay," Lisa reassured her daughter and son. "Your father should be home tomorrow. It will be good to see him.

"That was Don Lawson. He says now that the Chinese navy has left, life should go back to normal."

"I hope so," Lori said. "I don't like seeing you cry."

"I'm sorry, Dear. Tell you what. It's a nice day. Why don't we take a walk? Some exercise would be good."

The three of them went out the front door and turned left on the sidewalk. The security detail's van door opened and a new officer, one they did not know, stepped out.

Skip was disappointed. He was hoping he and Savali could talk. He fell in line behind his mother and had little to say. Neither did Lisa nor Lori. For the Bonners it was a time for private thoughts and reflections.

Chapter 26

Nightmare

The next morning the US flotilla arrived in Puget Sound and anchored off Bremerton. Shortly after the fleet dropped anchor, a small launch left the flagship, the USS Ticonderoga, motored across Elliott Bay to the Seattle waterfront. When the launch reached a dock, a ladder was dropped, and a young officer climbed up to be greeted by Don Lawson.

The officer introduced himself, Captain Tom Longoria, and told Don to take him to Governor James Bonner. He declined to shake hands with Don, which struck the administrative officer as both strange and unfriendly. Don ordered a government car and the two men and a sailor drove to the Dominion's headquarters building.

Don phoned James from the car to report the group was on its way. Otherwise there was no conversation as the officer viewed buildings still showing earthquake damage and small numbers of pedestrians making their way up and down steep streets leading to the unrepaired collapse of Interstate 5 tunnel ceilings.

James was waiting for them, dressed in a blue suit, red necktie and white shirt he kept in the downtown office for surprises such as this visit.

When Don led Longoria into the executive office, James greeted them with a smile that was not returned. Longoria told James Admiral Thurston wanted to see him and he would escort James to see the admiral aboard the Ticonderoga.

"Sure," James replied. "Give me a few minutes to gather some papers I'd like the admiral to see."

"That won't be necessary. The admiral wants to see you now and a helicopter is on its way to take us back to the ship. Five minutes later the chopper arrived and landed on the upper deck of a parking garage Don had ordered cleared. As the helicopter rose into the sky and turned west toward Bremerton, a worried Don Lawson watched it go west with a growing concern.

He immediately phoned Lisa who he knew after yesterday's troubled phone call was waiting and expecting to see James at home.

"Lisa, I don't like the way we just encountered the US Navy. Something's not right." After pausing for a moment, he continued, "For your safety I think it might be best if you and the children left town for a few days. I want you and the kids to take the 5 o'clock train from Tacoma down to Portland and return to Forest Grove. Savali Fautanu will go with you. I just feel the return of the US Navy might not be the blessing we all anticipated it would be."

"Don, why the urgency?"

"I can't give you a straight answer. I don't have one, but the way James was issued an order to report to Admiral Thurston disturbs me."

"Don, do one thing for me. Keep me updated in real time. I'm really, really disappointed James did not come home today as you told me he would yesterday."

"Lisa, I promise you I will."

Lisa clicked off the cell phone and went out the front door to the security detail parked at the curb. Reaching the car, she saw Savali put down his phone and roll down the window.

"I'll get Lori and Skip at school and bring them straight home," he said.

Lisa thanked Savali and returned inside to start packing suitcases thinking the family might be in Forest Grove for a week at least. The four of them reached Tacoma in time to catch the southbound train.

Meanwhile James and Captain Longoria landed on a helipad on a tender near the USS *Ticonderoga*. Five minutes later that were aboard the guided missile cruiser that served as Admiral Thurston's flagship. Soon they reached the officers' mess where Thurston awaited them. He was seated behind a desk and pointedly did not ask James to take a seat. Longoria stood next to him.

"James Bonner, on orders of the President of the United States, I am placing you under arrest. The charge is insurrection and treason. You will be held in this ship's brig until I receive further instructions from Washington."

"Wait a minute," James replied, stunned by what he had just heard. "I came here as a duly elected public official."

"Nonsense," the admiral retorted. "You have set up a government on US territory in violation of the laws of the United States. Look at that goddamned flag out there on the pier. Cut out the crap, Bonner. I don't have the time or patience to listen to you. You are on the way to the brig."

Two sailors seized James's arms, bending them back so he could be handcuffed. As they led James away he heard the admiral.

"Longoria, go back on shore and rip down that flag. Bring it back to the ship as evidence and run up the Stars and Stripes. These people need to know the US Government is back in charge and they damn well better understand it."

When James reached the brig, two Shore Patrol members took his clothes, watch, wallet and keys and gave him an orange jump suit to put on. They placed him in a cell, locked him in and departed.

James sunk down on a hard bunk and tried to gather his thoughts.

What happens now? He asked himself. His thoughts turned to Lisa, Lori and Skip. Will they also be seized? Don Lawson, too, along with the rest of Columbia's government?

Several hours went by. A sailor brought him a hamburger and

fries and a bottle of water. After more time, two sailors entered his cell, handcuffed him again and led him down a hallway to a hatch on the side of the ship. They walked him across a gangway to another ship. It seemed smaller, but James did not get a good look. It was night. There was no moon.

Within minutes he was back in a cell and heard the metal door clang behind them. He heard new noises and realized the ship was moving. Hours later he sensed the ship was encountering ocean swells, probably the Strait of Juan de Fuca, he guessed. Eventually he fell asleep.

When he awoke, the two sailors who had been in an adjoining cell were gone. The ship's movement indicated it was on the ocean. Sailors who monitored him volunteered no information. They brought him food on a tray, slid it through a narrow opening and left. James slept off and on, totally losing track of time.

At one point, maybe a day or two later, a storm swept over the Pacific causing the ship to roll back and forth violently as it continued its journey. The sailors who monitored him told him nothing.

James slept as best he could and did calisthenics when the roll of the ship permitted. He was bored out of his mind and was offered no reading material. In his mind he started thinking about what he would say when offered a chance to defend himself and his record over the past six years. It was an exercise he refined in his mind hour after hour. He also found himself praying, primarily for his wife and children. Surely Don Lawson had taken steps to keep them out of the Navy's clutches.

* * *

JAMES WAS HALF DOZING WHEN HE NOTICED A CHANGE IN THE ship's movements. The swells were gone, and the ship's engines noticeably slowed until they came to a full stop.

A half-hour later, two Shore Patrol seamen appeared before his cell, unlocked the door and handcuffed him. Then they led him to the deck of the ship and directed him down a gangway that led to solid ground and propelled him toward a helicopter warming up with its blades already turning slowly. It was night and overcast. On one horizon he saw lights which he presumed were a city. Pushing his head down to protect him from the rotating blades, the Shore Patrol escorts shoved him into the copter and told him to sit down on a bench. After climbing aboard and taking seats themselves, the door of the helicopter closed and it rose into the sky.

It was a short trip. The helicopter landed outside a hangar and was towed into a larger hanger. Once stopped, the chopper's door reopened, and two new sailors appeared. They walked him a short distance to a waiting Lear jet. Inside the Lear the pilot and copilot were finishing their preflight checks as the sailors pushed James up steps into a cabin. They then handcuffed him to the middle of three seats at the back of the cabin. They sat in two seats on the side walls of the cabin and fastened their seat belts. James saw the entry stairs retracted as the small jet's door closed.

I always wanted to fly in a small jet, he thought, but not under these circumstances and not without knowing the destination.

When the jet reached cruising altitude one of the sailors undid his handcuffs and asked him if he would like some coffee. He said he would and took a cup that was half full. The coffee came from a thermos and tasted a little bitter, but James savored it as he saw a rising sun peak over the horizon.

"Where are we going?" he asked.

"East Coast," the sailor who poured the coffee replied. "Andrews Air Force Base outside Washington, D.C., after we refuel at Offutt," the second sailor volunteered.

James shifted himself so he could look out one of the small jet's circular windows. He found himself looking down on a desert and mountain landscape, the latter showing traces of snow. Gradually the deserts below were replaced by higher mountains which in turn were replaced by plains featuring green irrigation circles. The Lear began its descent and landed smoothly at Offutt Air Force base west of Omaha and taxied into a hanger.

Handcuffed again, the sailors led him to a restroom where he relieved himself after an initial challenge of unzipping himself while wearing handcuffs. The sailors then led him to a vending machine where James bought a ham sandwich, a Dr. Pepper and some chips. The trio then returned to the Lear which had refueled and was waiting for them along with a new pilot and copilot.

When the plane reached Andrews, the handcuffs went back on. When it came to a halt, two Marines came on board and led James a few feet away to a panel truck with no windows behind its front seat. They chained him to a bench and the driver headed west toward Washington, D.C. and across the Potomac into Virginia. Seated away from the windows, James did not see the charred ruins of the capitol and Supreme Court buildings, residues of the final riots that had ended civilian government and the 1787 Constitution two years earlier. The van passed through a military checkpoint and came to a halt.

James was greeted by a Marine officer when he stepped out of the van. "Welcome to Quantico, Governor," the officer said as he led James into a building and down a hallway to his waiting cell. Fortunately, the building was air conditioned and James was glad to get out of the stifling combination of heat and humidity he encountered when he stepped out of the Lear at Andrews. His new cell was twice the size of the one that housed him aboard the ship and featured a table and chair in addition to a thin mattress cot and lidless jail toilet.

An officer removed James's handcuffs and told him a meal would be coming shortly and he would soon meet an attorney appointed by the Judge Advocate General's office who would represent him in court. The court would be a military court, not a civilian one. The officer then left him, and he contemplated his surroundings: no TV, no phone, no radio, although James could hear the broadcast of music coming from elsewhere in the building. Again, he was left with his thoughts. They were not pleasant.

                                * * *

THE NEXT MORNING AT 9 A.M. TWO MARINES UNLOCKED
James's cell door and escorted him through several hallways to a small
meeting room. Awaiting him was a Navy officer in an open-shirt
khaki uniform. The officer rose from a chair, extended his right hand,
and introduced himself.

"I'm LT JG Sam Watson. I will be your defense counsel in your
forthcoming trial." James shook his hands. Both men then sat down
on opposite sides of a small table and James initiated
the conversation.

"Tell me something about yourself," he said. "How old are you?
How long have you been practicing law?"

"I'm 26. I have been practicing law for seven months. I was in
NROTC while taking prelaw. It turns out I have a real problem with
seasickness, so the Navy sent me to law school. You are my first
major case."

"Well, Watson, maybe you can tell me why the Navy shanghaied
me and in secret brought me across the continent to Quantico? That's
where I believe I am. Before the trip I appeared briefly before an
Admiral Thurston who mentioned a charge of treason, which is
ridiculous. I am a duly elected governor."

"The charge against you is treason," Watson replied. "You led a
foreign government on US soil in an open rebellion against the
United States of America. You did serve as governor, but of a foreign
country set up in Washington, Oregon and Idaho in an open rebellion against the United States of America.

"That's bullshit, Watson. No one rebelled. The United States
government walked away from the Pacific Northwest. That includes
the US Navy who pulled its ships out of Puget Sound, locked up its
nuclear sub base and abandoned its air station on Whidbey Island.
No one rebelled. We did set up a drone force to monitor our borders."

There was silence, so he tried a different angle. "Okay, you are
my defense lawyer; so what's my defense?"

"Treason is a crime punishable by death. Your best course of action is to enter a plea of guilty and throw yourself on the mercy of the court and ask for life in prison."

James took a minute to absorb this information. After a minute, he asked, "Where will this trial take place? Will a jury be involved and how will it be chosen?"

"No civilian jury. Under the new US Constitution trials for treason are conducted in a military court. Your jury will be five high-ranking military officers. The trial will be conducted in this building. The whole procedure will be secret—including your execution if the court finds you guilty."

"Will I have an opportunity to say anything, to introduce witnesses in my behalf?

"Members of the court may ask questions. You may respond or remain silent. You will not be able to summon witnesses."

"Watson, I do have a question I hope you can answer, and a request. Are the American people really allowing this to happen? Are they putting up with a total loss of fairness and justice? What you are describing sounds like Nazi Germany or Soviet Russia. It's not the United States I grew up in.

"Also, can I contact my wife and family?"

"Bonner, the United States has undergone total anarchy which started before your earthquake and before you launched your country of Columbia. When the situation spun out of control, rioting swept through major cities across the country. The military stepped in and restored order. Anarchy has stopped. There is a new constitution which reflects the new order. With few exceptions, which were crushed by overwhelming force, the people have accepted the new reality.

"As for contacting your wife, that cannot happen. Secrecy is the order of the day and will remain so."

Watson arose, signaling the session was at an end.

"One last thing," he said as he turned to open the door. "Your trial will be the day after tomorrow."

Chapter 27

Are We Next?

WHEN JAMES FAILED TO APPEAR AFTER TWO HOURS, DON Lawson phoned the USS Ticonderoga and asked for Admiral Thurston's extension. A young officer told him his call would be returned, but in the following hour it wasn't. His concern growing, Don reached for a note pad and started writing down names. Thirty minutes later, still with no word from the admiral or a subordinate, he started making phone calls.

Two hours later cars started arriving in the driveway of the home of one of Don's longtime friends. The home fronted Lake Sammamish just off I-90 in the Cascade foothills. Drinks were poured. Some snacks were produced and shared as the group gathered in the living room of the home which faced west toward the lake and the distant Olympic Mountains. The sun was starting to set.

Don did a mental roll call, looked around the room and was pleased to see all but one of the people he had called were present. He set his glass down and rose to his feet. Seated around him were Lt. Governor Henry Brewster, Legislative Realist Party leader Alex Deane and his opposition counterpart Bridget Andersen, National Guard Commander Frank Chou, Dominion Treasurer Laura Nunn,

Communications Director Carla Haley and Social Services Director Dan Parker. Missing was Amy Cortez, director of State Relations and liaison to the governors of Washington, Oregon, Idaho and the premier of British Columbia.

"I've called you together because we are facing a crisis, probably the greatest one in the Dominion's history so far," he began.

"You all can see we are missing our leader, James Bonner. After the US Navy arrived this morning James was summoned—not invited—to appear before Admiral Samuel Thurston. He was taken aboard Thurston's flagship and hasn't been seen since. Phone calls checking up on him have not been returned. I have called this meeting to determine how you think we should react."

With that he took a seat and picked up his glass of scotch for a long sip. A long minute went by, the only sound in the room came from a grandfather clock clicking in the corner.

"Do you think Thurston will come after us?" Frank Chou asked.

"I don't know him personally, but from what I've heard he has a reputation of being an arrogant son-of-a-bitch. Frankly I think he wants to put the Dominion out of business," Carly Haley offered.

"That makes you, Laura, an especially tempting target. You manage the money."

A half-hour of additional comments followed. Don Lawson felt it was time to reenter the conversation and start focusing on a course of action. "If they seized James, each one of us could be on Thurston's target list. If he bagged us all, the Dominion would be amputated at the neck.

"I think Don's right. I think our best course of action is to get as far away from the US Navy as we possibly can. The same for our families. He might take them hostage to force us into his clutches."

"So where should we go?" Chou asked.

"British Columbia," Alex Deane said. "Thurston would think twice about sending the US military across the Canadian border. With everything going on, the last thing anyone in Washington, D.C. needs right now is pissing off Canada. The French in Quebec might retaliate by shutting off the lights on the East Coast." Deane smiled at the thought.

"Okay, B.C. it is," Don Lawson summarized. Let's get ourselves and our families as far from Puget Sound asap. I will notify Any Cortez and have her let the governors of Idaho, Washington and Oregon know. I'll also make sure Victoria knows we're coming.

"Frank, one additional task for you. Thurston knows about our drones and our capacity to produce them down in the Columbia Gorge. Let's hide them, preferably in places with lots of trees and lousy airstrips. Let's also try to move vital sensitive manufacturing equipment and our top engineers to Idaho."

The group broke up, but Henry Brewster stayed behind.

"Don, I'm resigning as lieutenant governor. I'm almost 74 and my health is not good. The strain in replacing James Bonner is more than I can handle. I hate to dump on you, but for me, this is the best course of action at this time."

Emptying his scotch glass, Don looked at Brewster.

"Henry, I'm sorry you feel this step is necessary. You have been strong and loyal since Day One. You have been steadfast since the Dominion was founded, especially when the pressure was on.

"I totally understand your request to step down. I hope your health stays strong. You will be missed by all of us.

"One last favor. Before we leave here, can you find some paper and put your resignation in writing for the record? While you are doing that, I will notify B.C. that we are all coming north.

"Even though you are resigning, Henry, I still think you and Margaret should come north with us. Maybe the two of you could find refuge in Revelstoke at that great hotel with the hot tub on the roof for skiers."

Don then poured himself another scotch and reached for his cell phone. He dreaded the call, but Lisa had to know all that had happened.

He caught up with her when she and Lori were out for a walk.

Lisa listened in silence as Don explained James's visit to the Ticonderoga and his failure to return.

"Frankly, Lisa, I don't know what we can do at this point except wait for the Navy to release information on James and his whereabouts.

"We want you to know the top Dominion officials are going to Canada. We want you to join us for your own safety."

"Don, they have James. Why would they want us, too? We had no direct involvement in the government. And, Don, the children are just beginning to reestablish friendships they had here when we moved north six years ago. I don't want to disrupt them again.

"I think we should be safe here especially if Savali stays with us. I feel very safe with him around. He is very protective."

"Savali stays with you," Don assured her. "I will want to talk to him as soon as I can. I will call you immediately when we receive any word about James."

"Don, thank you."

"Lisa, you call me if you need anything."

"I will."

Chapter 28

In Loco Parentis

Savali Fautanu found his mission more challenging than he first thought it would be once the Bonners reached Forest Grove.

He helped Lisa find and settle into a furnished rental house a few blocks from the home she and James had sold after their third year in Seattle. It was smaller, so Lori and Skip shared the master bedroom while Lisa took the smaller second one. Savali set up a rented bed in what had been the dining room of the house. It enabled him to see the front and one side yard.

The days passed slowly as they awaited word on James which never came. School let out for summer vacation. Savali gradually noticed Lisa was spending much of her days in front of a television set watching the two commercial stations which were back on the air in Portland. Lori discovered she and her old friends had drifted apart since they had been separated for six years. Skip was doing a lot of wandering around the town by himself which bothered Savali, whose mission was keeping track of all three Bonners.

Savali had notified the Forest Grove police and Washington County sheriff's office to let them know the Bonner family had returned to Forest Grove. As the days went by each of the Bonners seemed to be withdrawing into themselves. Other than the two daily phone calls—one to Lisa, the other to Savali—from Don Lawson, there was little contact with the outside world.

Two weeks after they arrived, Don Lawson told Savali the Oregon National Guard had a surplus Jeep he was welcome to use and he could pick it up at Camp Withycombe in Milwaukie. Savali made the trip the following Monday and with several bridges still down over the Willamette River, the round trip took most of the day.

Savali was almost back in Forest Grove when he received a call from Lisa who was frantic. Skip had been gone all afternoon and had not returned home for supper. As soon as he was back in Forest Grove, Savali crisscrossed the street grid south of Pacific Avenue searching for Skip without success.

Savali then phoned Mike Riley, Forest Grove's police chief, asking advice and help. Riley said he would notify Juanita Ross, his lone officer on patrol. He then threw in a random comment.

"One place I hope you don't find him is down on 22nd in the cold storage warehouse area. That's where the 'loser' teenagers hang out. Twice we've caught them there with illegal drugs."

Savali turned the jeep toward the warehouse area and turned on 22nd. A block later he spotted a group of teens lounging on a loading dock. They appeared to be smoking. Sure enough he saw Skip, noticeably younger than the rest of the group, with them.

"Damn," he muttered. He drove the Jeep to the back side of the warehouse away from the teens, parked it and walked up the side of the two-story building toward the group. Rounding a second corner, he surprised the group, including Skip, who clearly was upset seeing the big Samoan so close and obviously not happy.

"Let's go, Skip," he said.

"No," Skip replied. "I'm with my friends. I want to stay here."

Savali grabbed Skip by the right arm. A marijuana joint fell from his mouth to the ground as he began to protest.

"Hey, asshole, turn him loose," the largest teen among the group demanded. He rose to his feet and lunged at Savali. Savali wheeled.

His left fist hit the challenger square in the jaw. The youth staggered backward and then collapsed on the ground.

"Back off," Savali thundered. He dragged Skip, protesting and stumbling, back to the Jeep and hoisted the kid into the passenger seat before starting around the front of the vehicle to the driver's side. He saw Skip get out and start walking toward the group they had just left.

Savali gave chase and soon caught Skip, obviously slowed by the marijuana. He then turned Skip back to the Jeep. This time he hand-cuffed Skip to the passenger seat and made his way back to the driver's side.

They drove six blocks. He pulled over to the curb, reached his cell phone and called Lisa.

"I found him. He's okay. Before I bring him home the two of us need to talk. We should be back at the house in an hour or so."

Placing the phone back in his pocket Savali drove west on Highway 8 and then Highway 6 into the Coast Range. Reaching a spot with a pull off, he halted the Jeep next to a stone block topped by a water faucet that drew fresh water from an underground spring.

Savali turned off the ignition and unlocked the handcuff that tied Skip's left wrist to the passenger seat.

"Now that both of us have had time to cool down, let's talk and see if we can get some things straight," Savali said.

"Skip, three years ago you saved me from prison when you insisted your Dad call the county prosecutor and tell them I was not the one who beat you senseless in that ravine. You kept me out of Walla Walla. I hope you understand what a gift you gave me."

Skip did not respond. Hands folded, he stared at his feet.

"I know the past few weeks have been hard. Your Dad vanishes and then you, your Mom and Lori, are bundled off to a sort of exile in a town where you are almost a total stranger. It's not the life any kid would ask for."

Skip turned his head and the two of them looked into the other's eyes for a moment. He then looked away and stayed silent.

Savali continued. "Where did you meet the three guys—I'd call them creeps—who convinced you to smoke some weed?"

"The convenience store on Pacific," Skip said. "They were hanging out in front of the store. They invited me to join them and try something new. I was bored, had nothing else to do and thought, why not? We walked across town to the cold storage warehouses, found a loading dock out of sight from traffic. They brought out the weed and we all lighted up. I choked at first, but then started feeling —I don't know—light-headed."

"Skip, do you realize you would be behind bars in Juvenile Hall if Chief Riley or one of his officers found you? Riley would have had to go to your house and tell your Mom you had been caught with marijuana and faced a minor in possession charge involving a controlled substance.

"Skip, would you really like to put your Mother through that?"

Skip shifted in the Jeep's seat, turned and faced Savali.

"I'm a worthless piece of shit. I know it," Skip said.

"You are not a worthless piece of shit. You are a Bonner whose Dad came from nowhere to lead a country. He and your Mom are great people who have raised you to be a man, not a pothead."

"I'm not a Bonner. I was adopted. I was dumped on a porch and abandoned."

"And James and Lisa took you in and raised you as their son. You are their son, Skip. They could not love you more if you were their flesh and blood. When you needed them most, they were there for you. They always will be there for you unless you cut them out of your life.

"One final thing. Don Lawson assigned me to protect you, your Mom and Lori from harm. I take that assignment seriously. I consider you my friend. I want you to consider me a friend, one who believes your welfare is a number-one priority.

"Has this talk been worthwhile, Skip?"

"It has. Thank you, Savali."

"Good. Go over to the fountain. The water's potable. You stink from the marijuana. Flush your mouth. And when we get back to the house, take a long, hot shower."

Arriving at the house Skip passed by his Mother and headed for the needed shower. Savali gave Lisa a brief report on the afternoon and told Lisa he and Skip had had a serious talk.

"I don't think this will happen again," he concluded.

"Thank you Savali. We are so fortunate to have you." She wrapped her arms around the big Samoan's waist and hugged him. Shocked, Savali returned the hug gently and comforted her as he realized she was crying.

Savali was right. Skip was done with marijuana and he started acting more grownup around her and Lori.

Chapter 29

Trial, Conviction, Death Sentence

At 9 a.m. two Marines appeared in front of James's cell, unlocked the doors, entered and placed shackles on his ankles and handcuffed his wrists. They then led James down several hallways, James shuffling short steps, to a room with a window, a long desk in front of five empty chairs and two smaller sets of tables and chairs. Watson greeted him and they sat down behind one of the small desks. The Marines removed his handcuffs and ankle shackles.

"Have you thought more about your plea?" Watson asked. "A guilty plea might save your life."

"I've thought about it a lot," James replied. "A guilty plea would be an absolute lie. I never betrayed the United States. The United States abandoned me and the Northwest. That's the truth."

"I don't think the court will be pleased with your response," Watson said.

The door opened and another officer, a Marine captain, entered the room. He greeted Watson, sat down behind the prosecution table, opened a small folder and pulled out a single sheet of paper.

"I hope this doesn't take long," the captain told Watson. "I have a tee time with my CO at Burning Tree at 11 a.m. and I'm looking forward to a good round. The weather today looks perfect."

James looked out the window and saw bright sunshine reflecting off the roof of a wood barracks a few yards away.

A side door of the room opened and a voice called out, "All rise." Four high-ranking military officers and a captain walked in briskly and took seats at the long table facing James, Watson and the prosecutor. At the center of the group was Army Major General Norville Young who introduced himself and then the court. Air Force Lt. General Martin Oleson and Navy Rear Admiral Gregory Smith sat on his right, Marine Lt. General Xavier Cortinez and Coast Guard Captain Ewell Ramsey on his left. All but Ramsey were stationed at the Pentagon. Because the Commandant of the Coast Guard was in Puerto Rico, Ramsey, based at Lewes, DE, replaced him.

"This court has convened to consider the case of James Cameron Bonner," General Young said. "The charge is treason against the United States of America by establishing a foreign government on US territory, the so-called Dominion of Columbia."

Young then looked at the prosecutor. "Captain Farwell, present your evidence."

Farwell described the rise of Columbia and its founding as an armed rebellion against the United States, a recitation long on rhetoric and short on reality. He described Bonner as the rebellion's ruler. James was struck by Farwell's not mentioning either the earthquake and the following total collapse of electric service across the region or the US military's subsequent total withdrawal from Washington and Oregon.

Farwell summarized his presentation by declaring James Bonner was guilty of treason and recommended the court order the punishment for treason—death—in this case. He then sat down, and General Young turned to Watson, the defense counsel.

"Lt. Watson."

Watson rose and told the court James Bonner pleads "not guilty." He then sat down.

James could not believe what he had just witnessed. He started to protest but was gaveled into silence by the presiding judge. James studied the faces of the five officers, all stone faced and staring straight ahead except for the Coast Guard Captain Ramsey, who squirmed in his seat.

"Do members of the court have questions for the defendant?" Young asked, looking directly at Ramsey with a facial expression that emphasized he did not want questions asked. Ramsey got Young's message. He lowered his eyes and looked down at the table.

Young ordered Watson and Bonner to stand. Shuffling papers, he found the one he wanted and read the court's verdict.

"James Bonner this court finds you guilty of the charge of treason. The law requires those found guilty of treason to be executed by firing squad and the court so orders."

With that Young rose and the other four judges joined him and left the room.

"I told you you should have pled guilty," Watson said. "Bonner, I could have asked you to testify in your own defense, but it would have done you no good and the waste of time would not be good for my career."

With that he left Bonner with the guards. One of them helped James stand up and they escorted him back to his cell, James shuffling along, his feet shackled.

Meanwhile a real conversation broke out among the five officers of the court in the hallway outside the courtroom. Ramsey, the junior officer, asked his fellow judges for a few more minutes of their time to discuss the death sentence just rendered.

"Maybe we should slow down on this execution," he said. "I got an email two days ago from a friend who is stationed in Grays Harbor, Washington, a base still operational in the Pacific Northwest. The word on the street is that the Navy seized Bonner and is hiding him. Suddenly Bonner is a captive hero and the Navy is the villain.

"My friend in Grays Harbor says the situation has become ugly in some communities and Admiral Thurston has asked Washington for several thousand soldiers to help him enforce martial law.

"If this disorder grows, it could lead to major problems for those now in power. When the public learns we executed a governor, might we eventually face a firing squad?"

A vigorous discussion followed. After 20 minutes General Young spoke.

"Ramsey might have a point," he said. "I will delay the execution for two weeks. By then we may have a clearer picture of what lies ahead."

No one mentioned this discussion to James as he waited in his cell. All he knew was that the execution did not occur when he thought it would, nor in the days and weeks to follow.

Chapter 30

Alcoholics Supplying Alcoholics

The name was a rip-off but Sam Chablonski didn't care. He bought the old warehouse for a song following the coronavirus pandemic, finally solved a series of roof leak problems and opened a bar. Two blocks from the King Street Station, he featured a breakfast menu 24 hours a day with a top-flight selection of brews and booze.

Chablonski guessed right. In spite of its location, it drew a loyal clientele who favored alcohol and as time went by had plenty of money to pour into his cash register. In time he bought an adjacent building and remodeled it into a low-cost hotel which gave drunken revelers a place to crash instead of risking a DUII or worse. If customers wanted to share a bed that was okay with Sam. The room rate was minimal, and they paid extra only when they left a room in a mess. The King County Health Department never cited him for a violation that cost more than a small fine. The "Hangover Hotel" just generated more revenue and a tidy profit.

All went well until the fifth month of the Navy-directed overthrow of the Dominion civilian government and imposition of martial law. Five sailors showed up at the bar well down the road to being totally drunk. Sam, viewing the entry area to the bar, smelled trouble.

So did "Tiny" Smithers, his on-duty 270-pound, all-muscle, Black door guard who tried to direct the sailors to the largely unoccupied restaurant portion of the premises. The sailors disagreed and tried to force their way past Tiny.

Sam eased his way from behind the bar, stopping long enough to pick up a baseball bat stored under the counter. Coming alongside Tiny, he told the sailors to take seats in the restaurant portion of the premises and asked what they wanted to drink.

"Who the fuck are you?" The biggest sailor in the group challenged Sam.

"Lower your voice, asshole," Sam replied. "I own this place and I'm ordering you to shut up and have a drink or better yet, just get out of here."

"Hey, old man," another sailor slurred. "We're the US Navy and this area is under martial law. So get out of our way or we'll shut this place down."

The sailors surged forward only to be met with a series of blows from Tiny and from Sam's billy club. The ruckus drew the attention of several bar patrons who came to Tiny and Sam's aid. Soon the sailors were outside on the sidewalk and street. A surge of patrons followed and soon the US Navy was in full retreat in direction of the railroad station, pursued by an angry mob which viewed the mayhem as payback for the hated martial law and the Naval force inflicting it.

The Navy retaliated the following day, ordering closure of all bars in Seattle and its suburbs. This did not improve the Navy's or martial law's standing in the community. The Navy started encountering disruptions in food supplied to the fleet, which in turn led to raids on supermarkets. Protests grew. Two newspapers and one television station were closed. Grumbling by the public increased, even reaching outposts like Morton and Sedro Wooley, Washington and Umatilla, Oregon, deep in the interior.

In Seattle the Navy closed Alcoholics Supplying Alcoholics and its satellite, Hangover Hotel. Under the Navy's direction the two buildings were shuttered and then leveled to the ground for being in violation of the city's structural safety requirements.

Sam Chablonski did not go under financially, however. His sister, a loan officer at Toronto Dominion's branch in Seattle, convinced him earlier to put his funds in her bank. When martial law was first declared she transferred Sam's money to Vancouver, B.C. When ASA closed, Sam took a vacation, following his money north. Once there he purchased a rundown neighborhood tavern in Richmond. He no longer had to worry about Admiral Sam Thurston and martial law imposed by the US Navy. His clientele differed from ASA, mainly oldsters and retirees who liked to drink in the morning. They never rioted.

Chapter 31

In the Dark of Night

Savali Fautanu was bored and ready for a change in his life. He appreciated the status he had in life, the responsibility for protecting the Dominion of Columbia governor's family and James Bonner's family were gracious and accommodating, but in quiet Forest Grove one uneventful day after another passed without anything breaking the routine.

He also longed for the companionship of his fellow Samoans. There were no Samoans in Forest Grove. Pacific University, long a magnet for drawing Hawaiians to Forest Grove, was barely keeping its doors open following the earthquake and collapse of regular air service between the Islands and the Mainland. Savali was thinking of contacting Don Lawson to see if he could be replaced on the Bonner assignment and return to duties on the Washington State Patrol. He knew martial law was creating big problems in the Puget Sound area, but he missed seeing his mother and his social life in Forest Grove was nonexistent.

All that changed on a warm summer night when Lori told Lisa she wanted to go to a new friend's house for the evening. Grace Martin's family lived up in Forest Heights, an upscale neighborhood on the west edge of town. Lisa had met the Martins and liked them. She asked Savali to drive Lori over at 7:15 p.m. Savali took her to the Martins and he and Lori agreed that he would return at 10 p.m. to bring her home.

When Savali returned at 10 p.m., Lori did not come out of the house. When he rang the doorbell, Grace's mother told him she had left 15 minutes early and decided to walk home since it was a nice night.

Angry at first for being blindsided, Savali retraced the road all the way to the middle school and then drove his old truck in a crisscross fashion around the streets after he reached Forest Grove's grid street pattern. Still, no sign of Lori. For Savali, fear replaced his initial anger.

And it grew as the minutes went by. He stopped the truck long enough to call Lisa, hoping that somehow Lori had reached the house. She wasn't there. As he placed his cell phone back in its receptacle, he saw a pickup truck veer around a corner three blocks away and turn west toward Forest Heights at a speed well above the limit.

On a gut-level hunch Savali started tailing the pickup, staying around three blocks behind. He followed the truck out the Gales Creek Highway to its junction with Oregon 6. It continued west toward the Coast Range summit.

Savali saw the truck suddenly slow and then turn into a dirt driveway on the south side of the highway and disappear into the forest. Savali slowed, marked the entry in his mind and continued to the next milepost marker. He then made a U-turn on the highway and returned east to the unmarked dirt trail leading into the woods. Easing his truck into the sidetrack, he stopped long enough to unlock a box and retrieve a taser stun gun and a revolver, carefully fastening them to his belt. He then doused his headlights and, after waiting long enough for his eyes to become accustomed to the see the dirt track under the forest canopy, started driving slowly forward in the dark.

After going roughly 200 yards he saw lights ahead and also

spotted a side opening in the trail. He backed his truck into the side road, parked and started walking toward a small cabin. He also saw the vehicle he had been trailing.

Savali walked slowly and softly looking for any movements outside the cabin. There were none so he quietly climbed the two steps leading to a covered porch and then was horrified to hear a scream. He recognized the voice—Lori's.

Throwing all caution aside Savali grabbed the taser and hurled himself against the door. It was unlocked and opened with a bang. He saw Lori spreadeagled on a bed in the middle of the room flanked by two big middle-aged men. One of them grabbed Lori's left breast and squeezed it, causing Lori to scream again. He thrust his penis into her open mouth.

Grabbing his taser Savali leaped across the room, jammed the taser into the man's back and fired. The man in turn screamed and fell backwards onto the floor. Savali vaulted across the bed and threw himself full force against the second man who, shocked, was trying to pull up his jeans.

Five hundred pounds of bone and muscle crashed to the cabin's floor, Savali on top and still wielding the taser. Savali found his target and fired again. The man—this one had a beard—moaned in pain. Savali got up, found a pair of handcuffs and dragged the man six feet across the floor to a heavy wood-burning stove. He handcuffed the man to a leg of the stove, then rose and went back to Lori who was sobbing uncontrollably.

Carefully and gently he wrapped Lori in a blanket along with her clothes and brassiere and lifted her over his shoulder. He went down the cabin steps and walked as fast as he could to his waiting truck. He paused when he saw the thugs' truck, turned and detoured toward it. Opening the driver's door, he reached in to see, if by any chance, a key had been left in the ignition. Again, Savali's hunch paid off. He reached in, grabbed the key and pocketed it. Resuming his walk to his waiting vehicle, he opened the passenger door and gently laid Lori on the seat. After buckling her in, he rounded the vehicle, climbed in and started the engine. Once beyond the clearing in front of the cabin, he switched on his headlights and sped down the dirt track back to Oregon 6.

Reaching the highway he phoned Lisa and reported he had found Lori, who was hurt. He told Lisa to douse the lights and have her and Skip wait for them in the back of the house.

Once there he pulled into the driveway and parked next to his National Guard police vehicle. With Skip's help they moved Lori to the police car and the four of them headed for the emergency room at St. Vincent's Hospital with police lights and sirens going strong. Nearing the hospital turnoff on Sunset Highway, he cut the siren and flashing lights and glided up to the ER entry silently.

Going inside Savali flashed his police badge and explained the identity of the patient had to remain a secret. The women working the front desk protested but gave way when Savali asked them if they wanted everyone in the room to die from automatic weapons fire or a bombing. He also convinced them to send a gurney to his car so Lori could see a doctor and receive medical help she desperately needed. Within minutes Lori was whisked to a waiting room bed and was being examined by a physician. Lisa meanwhile gave the front office staff enough information to convince them they were not dealing with a charity case.

With Lisa and Skip staying with Lori or seated in chairs just outside her room, Savali returned to the police car, drove it to the hospital's main garage and parked it. He then made two phone calls. The first was to the sheriff's office. He told the shift commander the location of the cabin, briefly described how he left the two thugs and warned they might be armed. He then phoned Don Lawson.

Amazingly, considering the still-spotty cell phone service, he reached Don and gave him a full report. "Savali, we have to move the family," Don concluded. "I'll call you back in the morning."

The call came early.

"Savali, I want you to drive the Bonners to Boise, Idaho. Take I-84. Keep the Bonners out of sight. After you cross the Snake River, stop at the rest stop at the top of the hill and phone me. I'll have detailed instructions for you."

Chapter 32

Quantico to Chesapeake

JAMES NEVER RECEIVED THE FIRING SQUAD SUMMONS HE WAS expecting after his trial. One day followed another with food brought to him precisely at 7:30 a.m., 12 noon and 5:30 p.m. The overhead lights were dimmed promptly at 8 p.m. and came back on at 6 a.m.

His guards obviously had been instructed not to talk to him. They followed orders. James requested reading material, then paper and pencil. One guard acknowledged his request by nodding, but neither the books nor writing material ever arrived. Once a week a hood was placed over his head and he was handcuffed and led to a shower. Taking a shower, he knew he was alone, one hand still cuffed. He was not hit or physically abused in any way, just ignored.

Lying on his bunk one afternoon he resumed thinking about his situation. It suddenly dawned on him. His captors were focusing on his mind, not his body. Gritting his teeth, he vowed they would not win that battle. He charted a daily routine. It included exercise in the morning and prayers for Lisa, Lori and Skip, for Don Lawson and his co-workers in the Dominion government, longtime friends from his youth and working days in Forest Grove.

He worked hard on his exercising. He ran in place in his cell, did pushups and gradually increased them in number. Salvaging napkins from his meals and hiding them under the mattress cover on his bunk, he started keeping track of the days.

James worried a lot, especially about his wife and children. Never religious in his early life, now he prayed to God, constantly asking for their safety and his unending desire to see them again.

"My oppressors won't break me," he vowed.

One morning when the guard came to his cell to collect the plastic plate and fork, the man spoke.

"Bonner, take a piss and shit. You are going on a trip," he said.

"To a firing quad?" James asked wondering why it was necessary to relieve his bladder or have a bowel movement if a firing squad was his destination.

The guard did not answer his question. "We don't like cleaning up messes" he said.

Firing squad, no. Guards cuffed James's hands and ankles and led him to a locked garage in which a parked panel truck with no windows behind the driver's seat awaited. Unlocking his ankle cuffs, they assisted him into the truck and locked him into a seat behind the driver. A screen blocked his ability to look out the truck's front window. Two guards climbed into the front of the vehicle. A third took a seat across from James. A weak dome light enabled James to examine the man's face. He seemed to be around 18 to 20 years old.

James heard a heavy wide garage door rise in its tracks and the truck moved forward into daylight. No one talked. A car radio played softly, the sound muffled so James could not hear words that were spoken. After 10 or 15 minutes or so the truck steadied into a highway speed. James guessed they were traveling on a limited access park way or possibly an interstate highway.

James lost track of time. After two or three hours the truck exited the highway and traveled down straight roads at a reduced speed. The truck slowed again and stopped long enough for the truck driver to say a few words to someone and then moved forward again before halting in another garage. After another metal door ran down its tracks, the truck motor's engine stopped and the three guards helped James out of the vehicle. He was a little wobbly at first, but regained his balance.

"Welcome to Chesapeake" read the sign at the entry of the prison from the enclosed garage, but James did not see it since the guards had placed a hood over his head. This time his feet were not shackled so he could walk normally through a series of hallways until halted at a cell door. The guards placed him inside the cell, unlocked his handcuffs and removed his hood. They told him a lunch would be coming and then left him to contemplate his new surroundings. James was surprised to see his new "home" had a window. He stood up to look outside through the bars and discovered a dense wood lay beyond an open space bordering the prison building itself. After a half-hour his lunch arrived, a ham sandwich wrapped in plastic. Removing the wrapper James decided the sandwich was well past its prime. He put it down, lay down and took a nap.

He woke up when his dinner meal arrived along with a small book, the prisoner's guide to the Chesapeake Naval Prison. James read the book as he ate and learned Chesapeake had been built as a medium-security prison. Its mission changed after the military junta came to power, crushed ongoing rioting along the eastern seaboard and needed to house thousands of rioters it had arrested. After a period of time the number of prisoners being housed shrank dramatically, but the junta wanted to keep those remaining away from the general public and so they remained hidden behind prison walls. Lately, a trickle of new prisoners arrived, mainly journalists who probed the junta's rule with a critical eye.

Thinking back, James recalled the Chinese admiral he had dealt with in Seattle and Beijing's crushing freedoms the British had fostered in Hong Kong.

All that seemed like ancient history now as James settled into a daily routine like the one he had in his first prison—exercise, prayers for his family and friends and for his eventual release, either by returning to society or death.

Chapter 33

Nebraska Says "No"

THE TEMPERATURE HAD ALREADY REACHED 75 DEGREES WHEN Nebraska Governor Marjorie Norris walked across H Street from the governor's mansion to the State Capitol and entered through the south doors using her personal key to the building.

Continuing past the ATM and a humming soft drink dispensary, she climbed the few steps to the main floor of the building and turned left to the two city-block-long corridor.

Striding purposefully, the 46-year-old Norris headed north at a brisk pace. She entered the rotunda area and passed Gucci Gulch where lobbyists gathered behind bullet-proof glass that separated the two-stories tall, one-house legislative chamber from the world and then continued north to the end of the corridor. Turning right, she proceeded down the north corridor overlooking downtown Lincoln and entered the governor's office. There she was greeted by Jerry Halvorson, her administrative assistant.

"Governor," Halvorson said, "Fort Belvoir called. The President wants to talk to you as soon as possible."

"I wonder what he wants," she mumbled to herself. It probably isn't good, she thought as she entered her office, tossed her purse on a chair and sat down to pick up a telephone.

Governor Norris was not a fan of the President, nor of the new military regime running the country. Nebraska, like much of the Heartland, had largely escaped the riots and chaos that followed the collapse of the federal government several years before. She always felt America would be better off if it had struggled along under the old democratic order.

She did not recognize the phone number Halvorson had given her. As a matter of habit she wrote it down twice, once on a note pad she kept in her desk, a second time when she entered it on her state cell phone.

She was astounded when the President came on the line. "Hello, Governor Norris. This is Robert Jones," the voice of the military junta's top leader and now de facto President of the United States, boomed.

"Governor, we have a problem. The Pacific Northwest is not cooperating with the martial law we instituted after we broke up a government called the Dominion of Columbia. We need more boots on the ground to enforce martial law in Oregon and Washington. I am directing you and other governors in the Plains States to call up their Army National Guards and their support units and send them to the Northwest under the command of Lt. General Edward Stanwood. The Pacific Northwest has to learn it is part of the United States and start obeying federal law. We need to teach these people a lesson.

"Can we count you to do your part?" Jones asked. "We'd like these units to be ready to move west in a week's time."

"General Jones, this is a decision I can't make alone. I'll get back to you tomorrow if not sooner, but first I have to talk to the commanding officers of the Guard here in Nebraska since they will be directing our effort.

"Incidentally," she added, "the budget the Legislature adopted in May provides no money to carry out this order so who is going to pay for it? Is the state expected to put up a substantial sum of money? I can't commit spending it without the Legislature's leadership buying in first."

Norris knew the new government based in Fort Belvoir was notorious for not paying its bills or delaying payments, a fact of life every Social Security recipient in Nebraska knew very well.

"Who else are you contacting on this?" she asked.

"Eight other governors including your neighbors," Jones said. "Listen Norris. Don't stall on this. This is a national emergency. We expect Nebraska to do its part. Get back to me by 9 a.m. Central Time tomorrow." Jones concluded the call by hanging up.

Marjorie Norris laid her phone down, stood up and gathered her thoughts. Walking over to a window, she looked out over downtown Lincoln. When the state's Democratic Party recruited her to run for governor two years ago, she never dreamed she would receive a call from the military junta in Washington D.C. ordering her to send the Nebraska National Guard to enforce martial law in the Pacific Northwest.

I need some good advice, she thought. She wrote down a short list of people she should contact before President Jones' order was shared with the public. Then she started making phone calls. Her short list: Herb Fangmeier, commanding general of the Nebraska National Guard, Rebecca Clay, speaker of the Legislature, and Dave Osterweis, chairman of the Legislature's budget committee.

"Meet me on the fourth hole of Grandpa Wood's Golf Course near Elmwood. Come alone. This is not about golf," she instructed them.

Fortunately all four of them were in or near Lincoln and an hour and a half later she handed out sandwiches and soft drinks in a grove of trees on one side of the fourth fairway at Grandpa Woods.

Once gathered, the governor spelled out President Jones' request, offered her thoughts and concluded with the answer she wanted to tell Jones.

"I want to say 'no.' The whole idea is stupid and I don't want to disrupt the lives of the Guardsmen and their families."

The other three present reached a consensus quickly. The Nebraska Guard should not be deployed as an army of occupation in Washington and Oregon.

"So far as I know, no governor has successfully turned down an order from the President of the United States since the Civil War. I'm not sure you can refuse the order," General Fangmeier said.

"And if you do, I'm worried about your personal safety. Wasn't the governor of Columbia, what was his name, James Bonner, kidnapped? I don't think he's been heard from since," Fangmeier noted.

The foursome agreed Marjorie Norris and her family had to disappear before President Jones was told 'no.' Details were worked out in 15 minutes and the golf game was completed.

When she reached the eighth hole, Speaker Clay telephoned her brother, an officer in the Nebraska Highway Patrol. Others in the small parties including Norris also made calls as they finished the round of golf. An hour and a half later Norris and her husband Bill Bortcher and their two daughters, Mary and Georgia, rendezvoused at Walmart, walked through the store and passed through additional doors leading to a covered loading dock. There they climbed into a Chevy panel truck with no windows and were driven out of town to I-80 westbound.

Hours later, the panel truck turned off I-80 at the last exit before the Wyoming border and headed south on a gravel road for two miles. It then turned onto a dirt road leading to a ranch house. Disembarking, they were greeted by the owners, Wilma and Sid Johnson, and invited in. Wilma offered her guests a light supper and then showed the girls a bedroom and they turned in.

Sid Johnson and Bill Bortcher walked downstairs to an office with bookshelves on one wall. Going to the bookcase he reached in and pulled out a copy of the *1981 Nebraska Blue Book*. Behind it was a metal button. Sid pushed the button and a portion of the bookcase rolled sideways into a wall revealing a tunnel.

"It leads to a Cold War missile silo," Sid explained. "Lights in the tunnel are motion activated. If you hear helicopters or see or hear several cars coming down the driveway, grab your wife and daughters and go into the tunnel. A button on the wall inside the tunnel will close the bookcase. Walk down the tunnel to the silo—it's about 200 yards long. At the end you will find a room with bunks, a microwave and small kitchen. Wilma went shopping in Pine Bluff this afternoon and bought enough groceries to last a week.

"Stay there until Wilma or I come and tell you it's safe to come out.

"By the way, we get our TV from Denver. Like everything else it's the center of the world out here. Unfortunately, we don't get Channel 16 (Nebraska Public TV), but you should be able to pick up Nebraska news on the FM dial on a radio upstairs."

With that, the Johnsons said goodbye and drove their Ford 250 to a nearby unoccupied house on the ranch. Silence descended on the prairie.

As daylight broke over Lincoln, a car pulled up in front of Jerry Halvorson's house east of the University of Nebraska campus. A man stepped out, went up to the house and rang the doorbell. Halvorson interrupted his shaving, went to the door and was handed an envelope. Halvorson thanked the man, opened the envelope and read his instructions from the governor. Quickly finishing his shaving, he dressed and drove to the Capitol. Once there he contacted Lt. Governor Ed Winlock and told him he was in charge.

Then he telephoned Fort Belvoir. "Nebraska says 'no,'" he told the President's assistant who answered the phone. He then phoned the governor's offices in six bordering states to tell them of Nebraska's decision and sat down to await the firestorm he expected next.

It was not long in coming. Three FBI agents stormed into his office.

"Where is she?" one of them thundered.

"I don't have a clue," Jerry responded. "I'd guess she's probably not in Lincoln."

Chapter 34

God Responds

PENELOPE PINCKNEY HAD NEVER BEEN IN THE LOCKED-OFF CELL block of the Chesapeake prison before today, when she was instructed to take a pressure washer and spray the unoccupied cells with a disinfectant.

Once a jailer had unlocked the door to the block and let her in, he relocked the door behind her. She put on her goggles, face mask and ear plugs and fired up the machine.

Slowly, but steadily the stoutly built Black woman worked her way down the cell block, cleaning each cell thoroughly. As she neared the end of the row she thought she heard a noise above the clatter of the machine and the water hitting individual back walls of each cell. At first she ignored it, but when she reached the third cell from the end of the block she realized someone was shouting.

Penelope switched off the pressure washer. This time she heard a man's voice: "What's going on?"

She walked down to the last cell and came face to face with James Bonner. Both were astonished to see each other.

"Who are you and what did you do to deserve an entire cell block?" she asked.

"I'm James Bonner, the governor of Columbia. The Navy kidnapped me a year ago, tried me and convicted me of being a traitor to the United States. They sentenced me to die, but they haven't gotten around to it—yet?" It occurred to James that this woman was the first person to talk to him since he entered the Marine brig in Quantico after his trial.

"Who are you and what are you doing here?" he asked.

"I'm Penelope Pinckney. I work for Edwards Cleaning Company down in Edenton, NC. The Navy hired the company to power wash parts of this building and the boss sent me."

"I'm glad they did. Tell me something about yourself and your life," James replied, thrilled to be having a conversation with a real person.

"Well, I was born and raised in South Carolina. My ancestors were slaves. I'm married to a good man and have three grown children. I've worked for Edwards Cleaning for eight years. I'm Christian and a member of the African Methodist Episcopal Church. What about you?"

"My name is James Bonner. I grew up in Oregon. I'm a builder/remodeler by trade. I got drafted into politics and wound up a governor after a catastrophic earthquake hit the Pacific Northwest and the US government abandoned the area. The Navy brought me to the east coast, tried me and sentenced me to death. So far I haven't faced a firing squad, but I have been held in isolation."

"You have family?"

"I do, a wife, Lisa, and two children, Lori and Skip whom I miss very, very much."

James realized tears were welling up in his eyes, something Penelope immediately recognized. Her heart softened.

"James Bonner, let me pray for you," she offered, placing both her hands through the bars so he could take them in his own.

"Dear Lord God, help this man. Let him be reunited with his wife and children. Let it happen soon and keep them all unharmed and well," she said.

They both heard the cell block door start to open and both pulled back their hands quickly.

"Are you done?" the guard now standing inside the cell block asked.

"Almost, I didn't know anyone was in here."

"There is no one in here," the guard said forcefully, "And woman, for your own good, remember that there is no one in here."

"I understand," Penelope said, gathering her pressure washer and accoutrements and following the guard through the cell block door. Leaving the building she reloaded her equipment in a small truck, drove past the guard gate and the entry and headed back to North Carolina.

She arrived back in Edenton after 5 p.m. The office was closed. She unloaded the truck and drove home, her mind heavy with the experience she had just had.

For two weeks she kept silent and brooded about her meeting with James Bonner. She didn't mention it to her boss because she felt doing so might backfire.

Finally she decided to go to her church pastor, Rev. Jamal Burt, and seek advice and peace of mind.

Burt was a veteran AME pastor in his early 60s. Raised in the midst of gun violence on Chicago's South Side as a youth, he opted for small rural churches in the South as an adult. He had served Penelope's congregation in North Carolina for 15 years.

When Penelope decided to talk to Pastor Burt she didn't hold back. She described her meeting with James Bonner in detail and added that she had continued praying to God after their meeting, asking that somehow his wife and children could learn he was alive and missed them terribly.

When she finished, the pastor and congregant sat quietly for five minutes. Then Pastor Burt took Penelope's hands in his and prayed, asking God for guidance.

Afterward Pastor Burt leaned back in his chair.

"Penelope, I believe God hears your prayers and will answer

them. I believe God wants James Bonner to know his wife and children are safe and also that he also wants to be reunited with him.

"The issue, Penelope, is how does this information reach his wife and children without harming you or anyone else. The issue is how to pull this off without leaving a trail.

"Did you say Bonner mentioned Forest Grove, Oregon when he talked to you?"

"I think he did.

"Okay. I have an old friend who pastors a church in Portland. He knows a lot more about Oregon than I do. I will try to reach him, explain the need for secrecy and see what he suggests."

"Pastor Jamal, that would be wonderful."

"I will call you when I have anything to report."

"Thank you very much."

As soon as Penelope had left his office Jamal Burt picked up his phone, picked up a copy of the registry listing AME churches in North America and dialed his old friend's church in Portland.

Happily, he reached his friend right away and then explained the purpose for the call.

"I remember James Bonner. A good man. I voted for him twice for governor of Columbia. I always felt good about that vote.

"Jamal, let me make some calls. I'll get back to you. I understand the importance of not leaving a trail back to you and the parishioner who came to you," his friend said.

His friend called all the churches in Forest Grove he could find. No luck. He then tried the churches in next door Cornelius including Hispanic churches. Again, no luck.

The next day he started calling churches in Hillsboro, the next town to the east. When he reached the Iglesia Christiana Discipelos he struck gold.

"I know the Bonners well. My husband Alex and James Bonner were business partners," the church secretary said.

"Can you get a message to them?"

"I don't know where they are. They're not in Forest Grove. Alex, my husband, might be able to help on this."

"Thank you, Ms. . . .?"

"Martinez. Rita Martinez."

"Again, thank you, Rita. I'll call back in a day or two to see if you've had any success."

Alex Martinez was able to help. He reached Don Lawson, still parked in British Columbia to avoid arrest by the Navy. Lawson was ecstatic when he heard the news about James.

"I'll notify them right away."

Don reached Lisa Bonner as she was preparing dinner.

"Lisa, great news. James is alive. He's in isolation in a prison somewhere, but the military junta's hold on the country is weakening. There is light at the end of the tunnel, Lisa, and it's getting brighter."

Chapter 35

A New Life in Boise

The Bonner family started a new life in Boise under a new name, Galbraith. Don Lawson's political connections paid off with important introductions that provided a good income, a nice home in an old established neighborhood and new friends for Lisa, Lori and Skip, now known as Tom Galbraith.

The security issue was solved by Savali Fautanu, the only Samoan in town, being reassigned to Washington State Patrol duties in Seattle. He was replaced by Rand Schofield, a detective with the Boise Police Department who rented a house across the street from the Bonner/Galbraith home in Hyde Park and blended into the neighborhood perfectly.

Lisa, now nearing her 40s, quickly found a job in the offices of Idaho Power Company, the utility serving the area. Still maintaining a good "figure" as she moved into middle age gracefully, she soon attracted male admirers who enjoyed her company and hoped for a more intimate connection. Skip, now Tom Galbraith, teased her about her burgeoning social life, asking her on one occasion if she felt she needed a chaperone to stay out of trouble.

Skip, now a freshman at Boise High School, was a social lion himself. Surrounded by adoring classmates, some very attractive and very well "built" females, he dated extensively, but behaved himself "circumspectly" as his mother demanded. He also was popular with his male classmates and developed new friendships easily.

Lori alone in the family kept largely to herself. Now Mary Galbraith, she kept a low profile at school while developing especially close relationships with two classmates, Pamela Bosley and Cheri Donaldson. Lisa, always monitoring her teenagers, liked both girls. She wondered why Lori did not have dates or boyfriends stopping by the house, but said nothing. It may be just a phase, she thought.

The new neighbors were all friendly. Over a few months some of them asked if the Bonner/Galbraiths were church members. Some invited Lisa and the children to attend Sunday services and they did. Eventually they started attending Redstone Christian Church after Skip was invited to join the church's soccer team during a coffee hour. The team was in last place in the league and Skip enjoyed both playing the game and his teammates. Once he settled in, the win-loss record improved.

Lisa also felt comfortable with the church's lack of theocratic rules and its expectation that each individual had a responsibility to live out Christ's dictate of "love your neighbor" in the best way he or she individually wished to pursue.

As Lisa reviewed her life in Boise eight months after renting the house in Hyde Park, she had few complaints other than she continued to miss James. She was not happy with Skip's academic performance in high school and struggled on how to motivate him to pay more attention to his grades. I really wish James were here, she thought night after night as she turned off the table lamp next to her bed.

Skip recently had found a new interest, body building, and focused on it along with the Tanner twins, fellow ninth graders who lived around the corner a block away. Skip, Cece and Homer would spend three hours a day three times a week at a gym located not far from the high school on the edge of downtown. The trio commuted by bicycle most of the time.

Skip earned money to pay the gym fees by doing odd jobs for neighbors, so Lisa did not interfere as long as he made an effort on school homework. Lisa did not see much change in Skip's body structure at first but gradually did observe his arms and body were getting thicker. This too will pass when a new interest comes along, she thought. She did appreciate Skip's growing ability to move heavy objects.

A new development arose following a water skiing trip to Arrowrock Reservoir on the Boise River.

"I just met the most wonderful girl," Skip gushed to his mother after returning from the outing.

Her name was Shirley Clark. She was a freshman at Borah High School across town on the "Bench." When Shirley came to the Bonner/Galbraith home the first time, Lisa liked the young girl immediately. She really appreciated Shirley's willingness to help her in the kitchen regardless of the task involved. She also appreciated that Shirley took her high school studies seriously and had a 3.9 grade point record to show for it. Maybe she can encourage Skip to study more, Lisa hoped.

Shirley's parents on the other hand were not enthusiastic about Skip. "All teenage boys have one thing in common when it comes to girls and it's not good," Shirley's father told her mother after first meeting Skip. "I don't want them alone," he added.

Skip intuitively felt Shirley's parents' caution where he was concerned. He was courteous and treated them both with respect.

"I don't think they like me," Skip told Lisa one day after he and Shirley had run into each other at a Basque festival downtown and he had offered to walk her home. Her mother vetoed the idea immediately and dispatched an Uber cab to retrieve her daughter.

"They are being protective of their daughter. Keep acting like a grownup when you are around them and let them see you treat

Shirley with respect. Eventually they'll come around," Lisa advised her son.

She and Skip had just finished this conversation when Don Lawson called to report James was alive and being held in Navy prison on the east coast.

"Thank God. Thank you, God," Lisa prayed as she put down her cell phone.

She immediately summoned Lori and Skip to hear the news.

"Our days as Galbraiths may be coming to an end," she told her children.

"For now, let's keep this to ourselves. I expect to hear more from Don Lawson. When I do, I'll let you know right away."

Chapter 36

The Governors Lead

The Nebraska National Guard never deployed to the Pacific Northwest. Nor did Guard units in six adjacent states.

Military junta President Jones federalized the Nebraska Guard less than two hours after receiving Governor Marjorie Norris's refusal of his original request. Governors in Kansas, Iowa, Missouri and South Dakota were less confrontational. They asked Jones to federalize their Guards, hoping to avoid being stuck with any of the massive costs a mobilization would require.

One by one the Guard units reported delays in assembling the personnel and equipment required to subdue the Pacific Northwest. The Union Pacific and Burlington Northern railroads reported problems in assembling the freight cars needed to transport tanks and other heavy equipment. Amtrak said it would have to halt passenger rail service on several major routes to provide the requested passenger cars needed to haul troops west.

The real problem was that no one outside Fort Belvoir's high command saw any need to put an army of occupation in Washington and Oregon. A new campus newspaper at Notre Dame University captured the thoughts of many with its headline: "A Really Dumb-Stupid Idea." No arrests followed.

As weeks went by, a general consensus slowly gained ground among the nation's governors that military rule at the federal level was growing less popular across the country. The failure to deploy an army of occupation in Washington and Oregon exposed a weakness that was impossible to ignore. Public support of military rule, very strong when it ended widespread rioting and chaos, was eroding rapidly. Governors from the east coast to Hawaii noticed. Someone had to lead an effort to restore civilian government, but no one stepped forward to lead the effort.

In past decades the nation's governors gathered in conferences on a regular schedule. They had not met for several years so when the idea appeared to reconvene a national conference it drew an immediate positive response among statehouses. Wyoming agreed to host the gathering in Grand Teton National Park. Governors from Washington, Oregon and Idaho, Oregon and Washington were urged to attend. All three immediately agreed to do so. They were accompanied by a military escort provided by Admiral Thurston whose primary assignment was to keep Fort Belvoir apprised of what the conference was doing.

Historically national governors conferences featured work sessions in the mornings, recreation in the afternoons and evenings with spouses and children. This conference was different. The governors came to work. Recreation was left to spouses and children who had made the trip.

After an initial day dealing with organizational matters, the governors convened in the great dining hall of Grand Teton Lodge at 9 a.m. on the second day. Outside the lodge the blue sky was cloudless. The snowcapped Tetons glistened across crystal clear Jenny Lake.

The overpowering scenery visible outside the glass wall of the lodge was matched by a collective will inside the building to end the military junta's grip on power.

Initial deliberations focused on shortcomings of the Constitution written in 1787 and the substitute written to suit the military junta. With 50 people participating, major faults were identified in both.

By the end of the day a consensus emerged that the 1787 constitution should be restored with changes. The junta's constitution should be scrapped. The conference chairman appointed a committee of five and directed it to prepare a list of suggested changes in the 1787 document. The committee in turn identified four topics: (1) Changes in Article I dealing with Congress. (2) Amending the Right to Bear Arms clause in the Bill of Rights. (3) Elimination of the Electoral College and (4) Adding a new article separating the conduct and timing of federal and state election processes. When the governors received the committee's list, they adopted a motion offered by Louisiana Governor Randy Lemoiux: borrow a page from 1787 and go into an executive session closed to the press and public including the military junta's observers. It passed without discussion. The governors rose, left the great chamber and reconvened in a no-windows conference room elsewhere in the building. Surrendering their cell phones at the door, they took an oath of silence on what was to follow and began deliberating.

Amazingly, those deliberations did remain secret. Two days later they emerged with proposals for amending the 1787 Constitution. Back in open session, they unanimously adopted a resolution to submit the proposed amendments to their respective legislatures for ratification in the form of three questions:

> (1) *Shall the Constitution imposed by the military junta be scrapped in its entirety and the 1787 Constitution as amended prior to 1975 by restored?*
>
> (2) *Shall the 1787 Constitution and its existing amendments be changed by adding the following language?*
> *—Members of the House of Representatives shall*

be elected for 4-year terms concurrent with the election of the President.

—The District of Columbia shall be represented by one senator elected for a 6-year term. The Senate shall elect its Presiding Officer.

—The Electoral College shall be abolished. The President and members of Congress shall be elected by receiving a majority of the votes cast in a federal election. If no candidate receives a majority of votes cast, a runoff election shall be conducted six weeks later with the two candidates receiving the highest number of votes in the first round advancing to the runoff.

—Elections of the President, U.S senators and representatives shall be conducted by a Federal Elections Commission of 15 members, not more than five of whom shall be members of one political party or its affiliated organizations. Members of the Commission shall serve for terms of eight years and be prohibited from seeking any elected federal office in the future. Federal elections shall be conducted on a day apart from elections for any state or local office. The Commission shall maintain a separate voter registration roll of citizens 18 years and older who are eligible to vote. It shall reapportion the House of Representatives among the states following each US census and shall regulate campaign finance expenditures in federal elections. When vacancies occur, the Commission shall schedule a special election to fill the vacancy.

(3) *Shall the Second Amendment (Right to Bear Arms) be revised to read as follows?*

—Every citizen of the United States shall have the

right to own a gun for purposes of self-defense or hunting of wild game as regulated by law.

—This right does not extend to weapons of war capable of firing multiple rounds or to mortars or artillery.

—The US Department of Justice shall maintain a registry of all persons owning guns in the United States.

—When a gun is used in committing a felony which results in death or injury to another person, the last registered owner of that gun shall be liable financially for deaths or injuries linked to that gun. Victims or their heirs may seek redress in a court of law.

—This liability originates with the manufacturer of every gun and includes businesses which sell guns to the public.

Prior to adjourning the Governors' Conference, all 50 governors pledged to submit the proposed changes to the 1787 Constitution to their respective legislatures as soon as possible. A steady stream of ratification followed.

Chapter 37

Free at Last

Ewell Ramsey had just returned from a difficult mission of preventing the landing of a hundred or more illegal migrants fleeing the latest round of riots and mayhem in the Caribbean.

The Navy had first spotted the old, decrepit freighter in international waters off Cape Hatteras and the Coast Guard had been called to forestall a sudden turn into US territorial waters south of the Maryland beach towns.

The situation changed when the ship radioed for help, saying it was taking on water and was in danger of sinking. A sudden change in weather featuring high winds made a bad situation worse. Three Coast Guard cutters steered the ship to a yacht basin on the south Delaware coast where it sheltered behind a breakwater. One hundred and twenty hopeful migrants were interned in a hastily built stockade. The ship's crew of 20 were confined to the vessel under Coast Guard supervision until the vessel's owners could be contacted and repair to the ship could be undertaken.

Ramsey, dead tired, took a beer from his apartment refrigerator, settled into his most comfortable chair and switched on the TV. A newscast was just beginning on WILM and the lead news story came from Dover. The Delaware Legislature had overwhelmingly approved a return to civilian rule under an amended 1787 Constitution. Delaware was the 22nd state to ratify a group of amendments submitted to the states by the nation's governors six weeks ago.

Ramsey immediately thought of James Bonner and his role in Bonner's treason trial. Was he eventually executed or was he still in jail on a charge of treason? I have to find out what happened, he thought.

After 20 minutes he reached his commanding officer who was hiking the Appalachian Trail with his family. The cell phone service was spotty and it took a while for Ramsey to explain he needed an emergency leave from his command to follow up on developments following a general court martial trial in which he had served as a judge more than a year ago.

With the cell phone service cutting in and out, his boss never quite understood what Ramsey was saying, but he did sense the urgency in his voice.

"Go ahead, Ramsey. Take care of it," he eventually barked into his cell phone.

"Thank you, Sir. I'll give you a full report when I'm done."

Ramsey then phoned Fort Belvoir in an effort to reach Army Major General Norville Young who had presided over the trial. Miracle upon miracle—he was able to reach Young who was attending a party hosted by Military Junta President Tom Jones.

"Sir, a return to civilian rule appears likely. Delaware ratified the revised Constitutional amendments today. I think those of us who tried James Bonner will be better off ourselves if the military frees Bonner rather than the public seeing him hauled out of a prison cell in front of television cameras."

Young, relaxed after his third class of Jack Daniels Bourbon of which he very fond, understood Ramsey at once.

"You're right, Ramsey. Bonner will need a presidential pardon." After a pause, he continued.

"I don't think Bonner ever faced a firing squad. We would have been notified if he had. I doubt he's still in Quantico.

"Ramsey, you are as on top of this situation as anybody. Find out where Bonner is. Go there. Before we turn him loose, make sure he is physically and mentally in shape to be released. I'll try to reach the Coast Guard's Commandant. He actually may be at this party. I'll make sure you are detached to handle this special, delicate assignment.

"Thank you, Sir. I believe I've handled the detachment from my unit, but it wouldn't hurt to have the Commandant approve it also."

"Ramsey, find out where Bonner is and go see him. As soon as you've done so, phone me back. I'll contact Tom Jones regarding a full pardon."

"Will do, Sir."

Ramsey started making phone calls to locate James Bonner. He encountered security walls and no information until he reached a friend in Annapolis who was cooperative. At 10 p.m. his friend phoned back and told him the Navy had transferred Bonner from Quantico to the Navy's prison in Chesapeake, Virginia. Ramsey thanked him, set his alarm clock for 3 a.m. and crashed on his bed, totally exhausted.

When the alarm on his watch went off at 3, he rose, shaved and dressed in his new full-dress-blue uniform. He found his car had enough gas to get to Chesapeake. Stopping only for coffee, he drove west to pick up US 13, turned left and headed for the Virginia Capes.

Arriving at Chesapeake, he told the guard station at the entry that he wanted to see the officer on duty at once. Inside the prison he told the lieutenant on duty he wanted the prisoner James Bonner to have a full physical starting no later than 7 a.m. and that he wanted to be present for the examination. He also asked Bonner be provided civilian clothes suitable for travel. Finally, he asked for a place to sleep.

James was shocked when a guard woke him at 6:15 and told him to shave. That was after the guard measured him around his chest and waist and then down the side of his foot from his crotch to his ankle. A half-hour later he returned with two other men, one clad in a dress-blue uniform James did not recognize and his cohort who introduced himself as a doctor. The doctor told James he was there to conduct a physical exam.

The doctor started off by taking James's blood pressure and then examined his eyes, ears, nose, throat and continued on down his torso to his feet and toes. All the while he kept asking James questions testing his memory and his thought processes.

While this was going on, James wondered about the officer in uniform who he felt he have met before.

Finally the doctor sat back and turned to the officer. "He seems fine to me. I don't see any reason he can't travel." The officer thanked him and the doctor collected his paraphernalia and walked back up the cell block to the door.

"Bonner, I'm Ewell Ramsey. You might remember I was one of the judges at your court martial trial last year.

"Today, I'm here on a happier note. President Jones has granted you a full pardon and it's my duty to return you to the Northwest. The Navy is providing a small jet for your flight back to Seattle. You should be there by early afternoon. You are a free man."

James sat down, stunned. Is this really happening? he wondered.

"Here are some clothes, Bonner. Let's see how they fit," Ramsey said.

A half-hour later they were in Ramsey's car, fortified with two cups of black coffee, James gripping the Presidential pardon he kept staring at. I really am going home, he thought, his happiness, even giddiness, growing by the minute as they sped north toward Norfolk.

There the two men boarded a Navy Lear jet. The plane's door closed and the Lear thundered down the runway, rising into the morning sky and aimed west toward its refueling stop in Wichita, Kansas. En route they learned the federal government had lifted the martial law order for Oregon and Washington.

When they refueled in Wichita, Ewell Ramsey received a text message.

"We just heard from your friend Don Lawson, James. He says to drop you off at Gowan Field in Boise, Idaho so our flight just got an hour shorter." During the trip the two men exchanged stories about their pasts, their families and other topics. James found he enjoyed talking with Ramsey.

The jet touched down at Gowan and taxied to the military base opposite Boise's 24-gate terminal. It was high noon Mountain Daylight Time.

When the jet's door opened Ramsey and James stepped out. James immediately was embraced by his long-time friend Don Lawson. The two gave each bear hugs. Both had teary eyes.

After brief introductions, Ewell Ramsey rebounded into the aircraft which then taxied to a fuel station operated for the Idaho National Guard.

Don and James climbed into an open convertible, Don taking a seat in the rear leaving the front passenger seat open for James.

"We have one unofficial public duty today, James. We are going to announce your return to Columbia by going to Bronco Stadium where a football game is about to start. We will go into the stadium and drive around the track after your presence is announced to the crowd. I anticipate cheering, a lot of it. Those attending this football season opener are already very happy martial law after a year of it.

"Once we start around the track, release your seat belt, stand and wave to the crowd. By 6 p.m. tonight every TV station in the Pacific Northwest will carry this drive around. The public will know you are out of prison and have returned. This will preclude any need for press conferences or other distractions in the next few days.

"Next comes the good part. You will be reunited with Lisa and the children and begin a weeklong vacation in a private place. You can catch up with your family, all of whom are doing well."

The drive to Bronco Stadium went quickly. The reception inside the filled to capacity stadium was spontaneous and joyous. Almost everyone in the stands rose to their feet as the car made the circuit. Don Lawson's publicity stunt worked. As the car left the stadium, the public address system announced Governor Bonner was on his way to reunite with his family.

Twelve minutes later Don and James pulled up in front of the Bonner home in Hyde Park. A small crowd of neighbors, alerted by other neighbors who were watching the Broncos' season opener, had gathered.

Inside the living room of the house James and Lisa embraced and kissed again and again. James and Lisa brought Lori into their circle.

"Daddy, Daddy, Daddy," Lori mumbled. "I thought this day would never come."

Suddenly James realized they were missing Skip.

"Where is our son?" he asked Lisa.

"I called him when you drove up. He wanted to finish mowing the Lamerouxs' lawn. He'll be here in a minute," she replied.

Sure enough, he was. Skip emerged from the back of the house where he had parked his bicycle. Storming into the living room, he threw his arms around James who responded by giving his son a bear hug.

"Hi, Dad. You're looking great," Skip observed, a big grin covering his face beneath his Prince Valiant hair style.

"You need a haircut, son."

"We'll talk about it. Shirley really likes it."

"Later," Don Lawson interrupted. "Bonners, your transportation has arrived. It's time to go."

The family went out the back door and climbed into a Honda SUV along with enough luggage to clothe them for a week. With Don Lawson at the wheel, the Honda edged its way slowly through the crowd, now 250 strong, and headed north and west. An unmarked police car followed behind.

Soon the two-vehicle convoy was headed north on Idaho 55, the road to McCall. Along the way Don explained that friends of his had volunteered their home in Garden Valley for the Bonner getaway. It was secluded, the South Fork of the Payette River on its north side, Payette National Forest on its west and south and a smattering of new vacation homes to the east. Don pulled into a circle drive which led downhill to a house partially hidden from the road. A Boise County deputy sheriff greeted them and helped the Bonners unload the SUV. He told the Bonners he would be parked at the head of the driveway blocking entry to the property. He asked them to call him or his replacement if they needed anything regardless of the hour, day or night.

"I'll contact you in a week," Don told James as he climbed back into the Honda for the drive back to Boise. He explained the owners had removed the television set and left a week's supply of food in its place.

"The house is heated by a nearby thermal spring," Don explained. "So is the swimming pool out back—96 degrees year-round, even when snow covers the ground."

With that he drove off to return to Seattle to shut down the Dominion of Columbia. The Bonners were alone by themselves.

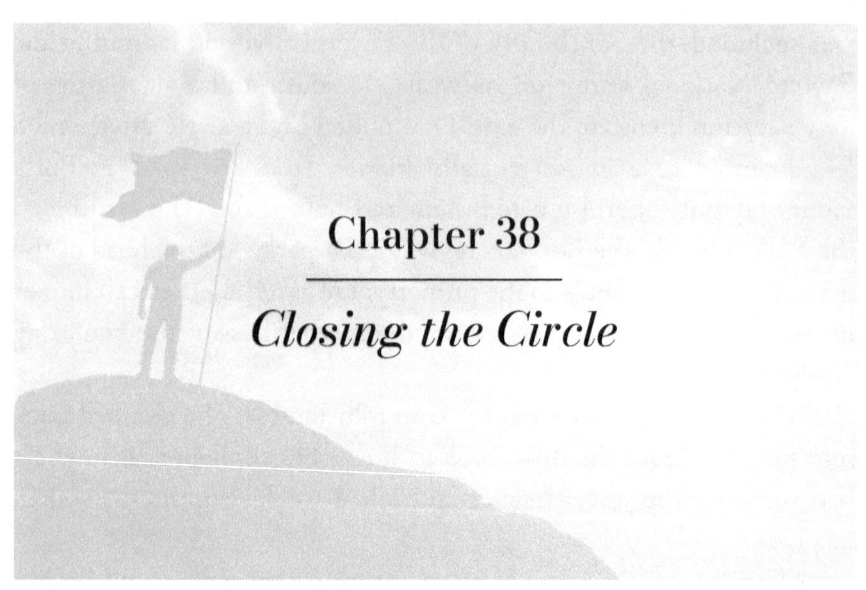

Chapter 38

Closing the Circle

The house the Bonners were to occupy for a week fascinated James. He had never seen so many 2x12 beams in such a small space. If someone knocked this house over on its side, it would retain its shape, he thought.

Lori was the first Bonner to discover a side benefit of heating the house with geothermal heat. When she sat down on the toilet in the ground floor bathroom, it was warm—heated by the 96-degree water in the bowl.

Exploring the drawers in a short hallway leading to a door on the north side of the house, Lisa found an array of swimming trunks. The Bonners decided to take advantage of the cache to swim in the pool a few yards outside the door. They soon were luxuriating in warm water—also 96 degrees. They splashed, swam and just lay in the soothing water for more than an hour before climbing out, showering and drying.

By now it was around 6 p.m. Lisa suggested they grill burgers on an outdoor grill and eat some prepared salad from the refrigerator. All four agreed that was a great idea. Skip and James emptied an open bag of charcoal and lighted it. The hamburgers, along with cheese for the grownups, disappeared along with the salad. The Bonners stayed outside, relaxing in the late summer evening air.

An hour later when James returned from a short trip inside the house, Skip called him over as he crouched down on his haunches.

"Come over Dad. Do me a favor. Sit on my shoulders," he instructed James.

"What are you going to do?

"Just do it. I'll show you."

James stood over Skip and sat down on his shoulders.

"Don't lean backwards. Stay on top of me."

James did as he was told and was astounded as Skip rose steadily without hesitating until he was standing erect. Skip pushed his father's ankles backward to center his weight and then walked 20 yards to the picnic stable, enabling James to step off onto a picnic table seat.

"My friends and I have been bodybuilding for over a year," Skip explained, a big grin on his face.

James was impressed. I'm not sure I'm strong enough to do this, he thought to himself.

Then a deeper thought. He had missed so much being separated from his family for the past year. I never want that to happen again, he vowed to himself.

One leisurely day after another followed, punctuated with the opportunity for James to have long talks with his wife and children. There was a lot of catching up to do.

At first he concentrated on Lisa, who seemed so much more independent and strong willed than he had remembered. He and Lisa quickly agreed that the family would remain in Boise, at least until Skip graduated from high school rather than return to Forest Grove. Her work at Idaho Power had drawn praise and the first of a series of promotions was under discussion by higher management. (In 15 years, she would be directing the corporate offices of Idaho Power and serve on the utility's board of directors).

After making all the parental decisions for a year while James was imprisoned Lisa made sure he was once again an equal partner in family matters. When they did disagree, which was rare, she still conveyed love and warmth.

They rediscovered the joys of sex when Skip convinced Lori to try golf at the resort across the river. Nine holes took 2 hours, 15 minutes which gave James and Lisa ample time to rediscover their physical attraction to each other. Their lovemaking was passionate and safe thanks to Lisa's careful storage of packages of condoms she had brought to Boise after the move from Des Moines two years before.

Lori discovered she enjoyed golf, which began on her third outing when she drove the ball 140 yards off the third tee and it rolled 10 yards farther than her brother's drive. Skip, smiling, told her to "quit showing off" and then congratulated her on her excellent drive.

James and Lori were taking a long walk down South Fork Road on the third day of their Garden Valley stay when James inquired about boys Lori dated.

"Dad," she replied. "Boys don't interest me. My closest friends are two girl friends. Dad, I'm a lesbian. I know I am."

James's mind reeled at this revelation. It took him a full minute to respond.

"Lori, if that's your choice . . ." Lori cut him off.

"Dad, it's not a matter of choice. It's reality. I've suspected it since I was 12 or 13. The night two men kidnapped me and tried to rape me did not change anything. Fortunately, Savali Fautanu rescued me. I avoided an unwanted pregnancy."

James was thunderstruck at this revelation. His first reaction was rage, first at the thought that Lori was assaulted. That was followed by anger at the Navy with took him away from his role as a father. His desire to know more about the attack on Lori was thwarted. Lori made it clear she did not want to discuss it.

"That's why Don Lawson moved us to Boise. He felt it would be much safer."

James refocused his mind on Lori's telling him she was a Lesbian. First he thanked her for bringing the subject up.

"Lori, I want you to know that whatever your sexual orientation is or whatever you do in life, you are still my daughter. You will always be my daughter and I love you with all my heart, soul, and mind. Never forget that. Lori."

He took her into his arms and hugged her tightly. Tears welled in both their eyes.

"Dad, I have been dreading telling you about my sexual orientation. I was so afraid you would do as many parents do, reject me on the spot and throw me out of your life."

"Lori, I've just spent a year of my life in prison, a forced exile. I don't ever want that to happen again. I want you close, as close as you want to be. You are always welcome in my life. Please believe that."

As they walked back up South Fork Road, James asked Lori if she had discussed her being a lesbian with her mother.

"No, I haven't. I was afraid to."

"Do you want me to break the news to Mom?"

"No, I'll do that. I would appreciate it if you would talk to Skip. The last thing I need is a stupid, smart-ass response from him. It would likely be the first words out of his mouth."

"I'll take care of Skip. I think he may be more mature than you give him credit for."

"Yeah, right. I'll always believe he will be a 'zinger slinger.'"

"Is that a teenage expression today? I have been out of touch for a while."

"No, I just made it up."

"So am I also a zinger slinger?"

"No, Dad. You're Mr. Awesome, Mr. Totally Awesome."

"I'll accept that," James smiled.

"You should, because you really are."

* * *

James sought out Skip once he and Lori reached the house.

"Sure, Dad. I was about to do my 3-mile run for the day, but I can do that later unless you want to take a break now after your walk with Lori."

"All I need is a half-hour. How long will your run take?"

"Forty-five minutes, maybe."

"Great, I'll be out back with Mom."

James poured himself some ice water and found Lisa deep in a novel on the porch overlooking the pool.

"How was your talk with Lori?" Lisa asked.

"We had a very serious talk, Lisa. She told me she was a lesbian and wanted me to know it. She also wanted to be the one to tell you and I promised I would not mention it."

"Don't blame yourself, Sweetheart. I asked a question. You answered truthfully.

"Actually. I've suspected it for some time. I was waiting for her to bring it up. I started thinking this was a possibility after she was attacked by the two thugs in Forest Grove. Savali rescued her from being raped."

"Lisa, what in hell happened?"

"Lori was abducted walking home from a friend's house one night and taken to a cabin in the Coast Range. Savali tracked the vehicle to a cabin and rescued her. That's why Don Lawson felt we should leave Forest Grove and had Savali bring us to Boise. He was worried about a Malvadoes link. We started here under new names and Savali went back to the Washington State Patrol.

"It's interesting she came out to you about her sexual orientation before she talked to me. I always thought we were really close."

"Maybe she thought I would react more strongly, be the tougher one to deal with. I did assure her that being a lesbian did nothing to change the fact that I love her very much and nothing will ever change that."

"She is worried about Skip's reaction. I told her I would handle Skip, which I will do when we take our walk this afternoon."

"Speaking of Skip, a lighter moment," Lisa said. "You're going to lose the battle over the length of his hair. His girl friend, Shirley, with whom he is very close, likes his hair just the way it is.

"Earlier this summer the three of us—Shirley, Skip and I—drove out into the desert south of town to watch a meteor shower. Skip set up a cot for me, laid out a blanket on the ground and lay down on his back, his head cradled in Shirley lap. She kept running her hands through his hair and massaging his shoulders."

"Why didn't you do that for me?"

"Hey, big guy, you've had a crewcut or very short hair ever since we met."

"Maybe our son is smarter than I am."

"I don't know about that, but he has longer hair and that's not going to change anytime soon."

James leaned over and pulled Lisa to him, giving her a long deep kiss.

"Do you love me with short hair?"

"I love you just the way you are. I wouldn't change a thing."

An hour later James realized he was having the best conversation he had ever had with Skip. The first topic was Skip's desire for a driver's license. "Mom's stalling on me," he whined.

"I think we can take care of that. Have you read the driver's manual so you can pass the test to get your permit?"

"I've memorized it."

"We'll schedule an appointment with the DMV. I'll check on car insurance."

"I've already done that. The permit does not impact car insurance. Once I have a driver's license there is a big impact. I told Mom I'd pay all or part of it."

After a minute or two of silence, James asked, "Who is Shirley? Tell me about her."

"Dad, she is the most wonderful girl in the world. She's beautiful.

She's smart. She's kind. I want her in my life now and always. And I think she feels the same way about me. Long term, I want a marriage as strong as you and Mom have.

"Dad, after you vanished and we moved here, several men wanted to date Mom. Mom was loyal to you. She never wavered. Even though we went a year not knowing whether you were dead or alive, Mom's love for you was steadfast.

"I remember one guy. A real creep. When he came back a third time and started toward the house I met him halfway and told him to get lost. I told him I'd beat the crap out of him if he came back again.

"Could you have done it?"

"I'm sure. He wasn't that big and I was motivated. I'd been body-building for almost a year. I could have done it. I think he realized it. Any way, he stopped stalking Mom." There was a moment of silence while that sank in, then Skip continued. "You know Dad," he smiled. "No one ever accused me of lacking self-confidence."

James laughed. "That's for sure. You can be a real smart-ass, always have been. Tell me more about Shirley?"

The young boy sighed. "She's the most beautiful girl in the world. She's totally fun to be around. We've been going steady for 14 months. There is only one problem: her Dad."

"How so?"

"Mr. Clark thinks the only thing I'm interested in is getting inside her pants."

"Well, you must have thought about it. Skip, you are at the age when your sex drive goes into high gear. I'm sure Shirley's father knows that." James recalled losing his virginity at age 16, but he didn't think discussing that right now would be a good idea.

Skip gave James an anguished look. "Dad, Shirley is not a one-night stand. I want her in my life forever. If I touched her in the wrong way, I'd lose her. I know I would.

"As far as Mr. Clark is concerned, I've been very respectful. I've been the same with Mrs. Clark. I don't know what else to do to convince them I'm as interested in Shirley's good reputation as they are."

The father and son walked 100 yards, each lost in his thoughts.

"Dad, do you have any advice for me?"

"Skip, I'd say keep doing the same thing you have been with her parents—be courteous, respectful. Offer to help her mother and dad when you think your help might be useful.

"By the way, what does Shirley's father do for a living?"

"He's a lawyer, I guess a very good and successful one. His family has a long history in Idaho politics. Shirley mentioned they have governorships and US senators in their past."

"You know Skip, I think there is something you can do to impress the Clarks. What was your grade point last semester?"

"I don't know, probably a high C or a B."

"I doubt if that impresses the Clarks when they think about who they want for a son-in-law or who they want Shirley dating in high school. Push your grades up to straight As and they'll respect you for it."

"That's a tall order. I'm not sure I'm smart enough."

"Is Shirley worth it, worth working for it?"

"Well, yes."

"Then do it. Skip, when you focus on something—your body-building is a good example—you go all out on it. So apply it to improving your grades.

"Besides, maybe you and Shirley could spend more time studying together."

James looked at Skip, who was smiling at him.

"Sometimes, Dad, you have a great idea."

"I try. I hope I can keep up with my son."

Suddenly, James stopped. "Skip there is something else I want to discuss with you. I had a talk with Lori today. She told me she's a lesbian. How do you feel about that?"

Skip shrugged. "I'm not surprised. Lori is a really good-looking girl, but no boy friends. I'm sure she could have a lot of them if she wanted."

"Dad, my generation doesn't have the hang-ups your generation has. I have gay friends. It's no big deal, at least in Boise High School. I do remember a row over transgender bathrooms last year. There was a big blow-up at the school board, but as far as the kids are concerned, the whole issue is stupid. When you need to take a piss, you take a piss."

"Would you tease Lori about being a lesbian?"

"A year or two ago I probably would have. Now I wouldn't think of it. It would hurt her. I don't want to hurt my sister. I'm sure Shirley would be mad at me if she found out I'd made some snide remark to put Lori down."

"Skip, do me a favor. When you and Lori are alone, tell her you understand she's a lesbian and that you're okay with that."

"Not a problem. I'll do it."

"Thanks."

Chapter 39

The Final Link

Lisa Bonner loved Saturday mornings, especially when it was warm enough to sit outside and drink her coffee while checking emails that had arrived since she left the office at 5 p.m. the day before.

This Saturday Lisa was on the front porch, shaded by a roof. She was glad she was protected from the sun. The day was going to be a hot one. Every home in Idaho Power's service territory would have its air conditioning going full blast—good for Idaho Power's revenues as long as the transmission network held together. The company's engineers had indicated it would.

A few neighbors walked by on their way to a nearby coffee shop popular with the locals. Vehicular traffic was sparse. Lori was still asleep. James and Skip were both at work, James visiting a home under construction in Hailey whose owner was upset with the Reece-Ames Construction Company's contractor building their two-story home. Skip was working a four-hour shift at Albertson's restocking shelves and corralling shopping carts shoppers had abandoned in the parking lots.

Lisa was surprised when a late-model Toyota parked in front of the Bonners' home and a middle-aged woman got out and walked up the sidewalk toward the porch. Lisa closed her laptop. "Can I help you?" she asked as the woman climbed the three steps and reached the porch.

"Mrs. Bonner, we were neighbors years ago in Forest Grove," the woman said.

Lisa invited the woman to sit down and offered her coffee. "No," the woman said, "but if you have tea, I'd appreciate a cup."

Lisa got up, went into the house, deposited the laptop and reached the kitchen where Lori, the only tea drinker in the house, kept her box of Stash teas.

"Do you have a preference?" She called out to the woman on the porch.

"Earl Grey if you have it. Otherwise, anything would be fine."

Lisa opened a packet, put the tea bag in a cup and waited a minute until water in a kettle reached the boiling point. She returned to the porch with a cup of steaming tea.

"I'm sorry. Forest Grove was many years ago. Your face I think I may have seen before, but I really don't remember you."

"I understand. We lived a block away from you. I recall waving to you when you went by my house pushing a baby stroller.

"Let me tell you why I'm here. My name is Ruthanne Smith. I'm the one who left a box on your front porch with a baby boy in it. He was 12 days old at the time. I lost track of you when you moved to Seattle and I moved out of Forest Grove.

"I'd like to see my son and be part of his life," she said.

Lisa was thunderstruck. Deep in heart she felt that someday whoever had left the infant on their front porch would surface, but her fear had dwindled as the years went by.

"When I saw Governor Bonner returning to Boise on TV a year ago, I started making inquiries," Ruthanne continued. "I thought you and your husband probably had moved back to Seattle. On a visit to Forest Grove I contacted his former business partner's company and learned you were living in Boise. So I moved here and today I found you."

Lisa tried to gather her thoughts, which took a few minutes.

"Ruthanne, why did you leave your baby on our front porch? Why would you do that?"

"I was afraid of my husband. He became vicious when he was drunk, and I worried he might kill Franklin in his cradle. He would beat me and throw objects at the wall. He was drunk often and when he was, he was totally out of control."

"Franklin? You named the baby Franklin?"

"Franklin Keohokalole. My husband Bert is half native Hawaiian so Franklin is one quarter native Hawaiian, and three quarters Haole, or white. At least we think he is. Genealogy is not something I've spent a lot of time studying."

Lisa let Ruthanne go on with her story, which was convoluted to say the least. Ruthanne had met Bert on the beach at Kona. They dated and eventually married, a move that caused Ruthanne's parents to disown her. They had never reconciled, even after a divorce ended her marriage.

Lisa broke into Ruthanne's monologue at one point.

"Ruthanne, you should know that James and I adopted the baby before we left Forest Grove. For months we had searched for his parents. The adoption was certified by the Washington County Circuit Court. Skip is our son by law."

"That may be at the case, but I still want to be part of his life and for him to be part of mine."

That sounded a little ominous to Lisa. She wished James was home. She knew Skip would be returning after finishing his shift at Albertson's. She wished she could tell him Ruthanne was on the front porch so he would not be totally blindsided. Skip usually turned off his cell phone until he had a break at Albertson's. She was not able to reach him.

When Skip rode his bicycle into the driveway, he smiled and waved to the two women on the porch as he proceeded to the backyard, parked the bike and walked into the house, allowing the screen door to slam shut.

A minute later the 16-year-old came out to the front porch. Ruthanne rushed to him, threw her arms around him and started crying.

"My son. My son. It's been so long." She gripped him even tighter.

Skip's face registered total shock. "Who are you?" he asked.

"I'm your mother. I brought you into the world, my beautiful child."

Skip's face registered total panic. Lisa saw her son, Mr. Totally-In-Control-At-All-Times, totally lose control. He was shaking. His arms hung down from his shoulders, weak, helpless.

Skip's eyes, registering terror, connected with Lisa. "Do something," he silently pleaded to the mother he had always known.

"Ruthanne, let's all sit down and collect our breaths," Lisa said quietly.

Ruthanne released Skip and took her seat. Skip collapsed into an empty chair. He stared at Ruthanne. His face still registering shock, imploring Lisa to work out something.

"Ruthanne, James, the father Skip has known all his life, will be back from Hailey this evening. The four of us can have dinner together and discuss this situation at length. Maybe we can chart a future satisfactory to all of us."

Skip found his voice. "Not tonight, Mom. Shirley and I already have plans."

"Plans," Ruthanne protested. "What could be more important than me being reunited with my son?"

"Skip. You and Shirley do what you planned to do this evening. The four of us can meet after church tomorrow and talk. Hopefully we can work out something we all can live with.

"And Ruthanne, in this household we honor our commitments. Skip has made a commitment for this evening. Once made, he'll do it."

Lisa then extended an invitation. "Ruthanne, we are members of Redstone Christian Church over on the Bench. Would you like to join us for the 11 o'clock service tomorrow? We could have lunch afterward.

"I'll pass on church," Ruthanne replied grumpily. "I don't do church."

Skip breathed a sigh of relief. The last thing he needed was to have this woman proclaiming she was his mother at church.

Ruthanne left the Bonners' after grilling Skip for half an hour about his activities, his hobbies, his studies, his friends.

She didn't learn much. Skip volunteered a minimal amount of information.

At that point, Lori came out of the house and Lisa introduced her to Ruthanne as "an old friend." After Ruthanne left, Lisa explained Ruthanne's presence in detail. She also told Lori that she herself could not have more children after she was born. The doctors had told her she probably would not survive giving birth a second time. She and James decided not to risk a second pregnancy.

Lori decided to skip the Bonners' second meeting with Ruthanne when the foursome gathered around 4 p.m. at Sunny Mountain Pizza on West State Street. The restaurant was quiet in the interim between lunch and dinner crowds and the Bonners' found a table for four in a quiet corner where their conversation would be private. James, Lisa and Skip had agreed on a plan for keeping the conversation constructive.

James took the lead. He asked Ruthanne to discuss her life after she placed her baby in a cardboard box and left it on the Bonners' porch. After some low-key probing, she described her life in detail: her divorce, her former husband's early death from liver failure, her secretarial jobs at several electrical public utility districts in eastern Washington.

James then steered the conversation toward Skip and the future.

He reminded Ruthanne that Skip would turn 18 in less than two years. He then would be a fully emancipated adult who legally would be in charge of all decisions affecting his life.

He went on to explain Skip—Michael Henry Bonner—already had a life. He had a job. He had a girlfriend he loved deeply. His future prospects were bright, especially after his grades in school had improved sharply in the past year.

"Ruthanne, Lisa and I learned a long time ago that if you treat a child or teenager like an adult he or she will respond as an adult. That's been our history with Skip. If you try to control him, he will resist and your relationship with him will never be close. Your best option in my view is to give him time and space to come to you."

At the end of the meal Ruthanne told the Bonners they probably were right. She would wait for Skip, her Franklin, to come to her. Cell phone numbers were exchanged, all except for Skip's.

Five months later Skip phoned Ruthanne. They agreed to meet in McCall 100 miles north of Boise where the Clarks had a vacation home. Skip brought Shirley with him. The three of them had a pleasant meal. Ruthanne hugged both Skip and Shirley when they parted.

"Take care of him, Shirley. He's precious. And you, you behave yourself," she told her son.

"I'll try," Skip replied, a big grin on his face.

When Skip graduated from Boise High, Ruthanne was invited to the ceremony and to the graduation party at the Bonners' that followed.

After graduation Skip decided to spend a year touring Europe and taking temporary jobs there before starting college. Shirley joined him for the first two months as they made their way through England, France and the Scandinavian countries.

Shirley flew home in September to begin her freshman year at Wellesley. Skip stayed in Europe, touring the Baltic countries and Poland. By Christmas he was in Ukraine, where he was invited to join the Denys Sychkov family in Uzghorod for the first of Ukraine's two traditional Christmas celebrations.

During their separation, Skip and Shirley communicated daily through texting and telephone calls. In Boise, the Bonners invited Ruthanne to join them for Christmas and she did.

At a predetermined time New Year's Day, Skip reunited with his family via Skype. Shirley, home for the holidays joined them. She alone was not surprised when Skip showed up on the computer screen with shoulder-length hair and a beard.

"Skip, you really, really do need a haircut," James said.

"I'll think about it, Dad," his son replied.

When the Skype meeting came to an end, Skip asked for a private minute or two with Shirley.

"Shirley, this trip has been great, but I miss you terribly. I will be home before summer. I never want to be away from you again."

"Skip, darling. I feel the same way. I will always want you by my side."

Chapter 40

Remembering Columbia

When Don Lawson left the reunited Bonner family in Idaho, he returned to Seattle and starting dismantling the Dominion of Columbia.

James Bonner's insistence of not having the Dominion take on long-term debt made his job relatively easy. Employees received final payments on salaries. Advertisements stated deadlines for contractors submitting final bills. Money left in the Dominion's treasury after this process was finished was returned to the three states and province. They in turn forwarded it to their citizens. Those checks, generally small, left the public feeling good about their one-time temporary country.

In six months Don made a trip to Boise to visit the Bonners and have James put his signature on final documents. These were archived in four separate collections which were delivered to historical societies in Washington, Oregon, Idaho and British Columbia.

Don's trip was special for another reason. His wife Agatha, whom the Bonners had not met, accompanied him.

Not long after, the Bonners hosted Savali Fautanu, who introduced him to his wife, Clara, and their first-born son, Bonner Fautanu.

The Bonner family shrank after Lori moved to Eugene to study philosophy at the University of Oregon. Back home from Europe Skip earned a bachelor's degree at Boise State University and learned he enjoyed selling commercial real estate. He joined a local firm.

Initially worried his Hawaiian blood might upset the Clarks, he learned that was not a concern. He and Shirley were married in Boise's Catholic cathedral, a wedding that drew 400 guests.

Skip and Shirley moved into their first home on Warm Springs Mesa and started raising a family that eventually included four children, all spoiled by their Clark and Bonner grandparents.

Nine years after James's release from prison, he received another call from Don Lawson.

"Jim, I'm getting requests to have a reunion of the Dominion government's leaders. Most think gathering in Revelstoke would be a great idea. Can you and Lisa break away next August 6th and join us for a few days? It should be a good party."

"Lisa and I would like to come on two conditions."

"Like what?"

"I give no speeches and no talk of another term as governor. I really am committed to a private lifestyle."

"I'm with you. No Chinese navy either."

They both laughed.

And they both enjoyed the reunion immensely. So did their spouses.

The reunion took on a special meaning for Lisa the morning after it ended when she and James were sharing a ham and cheese omelet in the Explorer's restaurant.

A couple appeared in front of them and the silver haired woman asked, "Are you James and Lisa Bonner?"

Told yes, the woman said she was Marjorie Norris.

"I was governor of Nebraska when the Navy kidnapped you, Governor Bonner. I turned down a Presidential order to call up the

Nebraska Guard to enforce martial law in Washington and Oregon. Knowing you had disappeared, my state officials made sure I didn't suffer the same fate."

The Bonners insisted Norris and her husband Bill Bortcher join them for breakfast. The foursome shared their experiences for two hours.

"Lisa, I especially have wanted to meet you for years. I can't imagine how you coped not knowing whether James was alive or dead for more than a year while raising two teenagers at the same time. You are a very strong woman."

"Well, thank you for your kind words and thoughts. That year apart from James was horrible in many ways, but my children helped me get through it. So did strong friends at church. God answered my prayers. Since then James and I have had nine wonderful years together. Today we have grandchildren close by. What a blessing.

"And Marjorie, thank you for joining us at breakfast. You have this a very, very special day for me.

"Finally, I hope we meet again."

About the Author

Harry Bodine was born in Houston, Texas, in 1932, and lived in the state until moving to suburban St. Louis, MO, in 1948. He graduated from the University of Missouri School of Journalism in 1954, served in the US Army (field artillery) as an officer in the US and Germany for two years.

He launched a forty-one-year career as a newspaper reporter and editor at the Roseburg, Oregon *News-Review* in 1956. After editing weekly papers in Oregon, Colorado, and Idaho, he joined the staff of *The Oregonian* in 1964. He worked there for thirty-one years, specializing in politics, and state and local government issues. He interviewed five US Presidents—Nixon through George H. W. Bush.

In 1986, he received Washington County's first Distinguished Service Award. Since retiring, he helped lead six campaigns for library service financing in Washington County, and served three years as a member and chairman of the Cedar Mill / Bethany libraries board of directors. The Oregon Library Association named him its statewide Library Volunteer Service Award.

Mr. Bodine and his wife, Winona, have been married sixty-one years. They raised two sons, one of whom survives. They have one granddaughter, newly commissioned as an officer in the US Air Force.

www.ingramcontent.com/pod-product-compliance
Lightning Source LLC
Chambersburg PA
CBHW031459160726
47994CB00005B/2100

9 798218 064099